This book is dedicated to my friends

WHEEL OF KARMA

Rob Alexander

JumpFish Publishing
Sydney

First published September 2025 by JumpFish Publishing.

This edition, November, 2025.

ISBN-13: 978-0-9945792-6-3

Copyright © 2025 JumpFish Publishing

9 8 7 6 5 4 3

A CIP catalogue record for this book is available from the Australian Library.

Printed and bound by Ingram Spark.

Acknowledgements

I extend my gratitude to the engineers who invented Large Language Models. They replaced the traditional discussions I used to have with real people, allowing me to workshop and refine the ideas in this story at my own convenience. Maybe the results are different because of that. I will leave it to the reader to decide. What is true is that I never let AI write the story. I directed the entire story from start to finish even though I accepted some sentences generated by AI simply because they did mostly what I wanted.

"By the 2030s, we will have the means to accomplish whole-brain emulation using nanobots. [...] In the 2040s, the nonbiological portion of our intelligence will exceed the biological portion. By 2045, we will have expanded intelligence a billion-fold by this means. [...] We will reach a point where our intelligence is so expanded that we will be able to design new forms of intelligence not bound by biology ..."

– Ray Kurzweil, *The Singularity Is Near,* (2005) –

– 1 –

Neon Ghosts

Shanghai, Pudong District. 2:17 a.m., 2047

THE RAIN fell in silver sheets across Pudong's streets, neon lights and holograms smearing into liquid color. Shanghai's heart had slowed to a murmur—the last finance workers stumbling home through puddles of shifting hues, their smart-glasses flickering with phantom alerts. Delivery drones hummed overhead like mechanical insects, ferrying late-night cravings to insomniacs in towering high-rises, their red strobes slicing through layered mist.

Lin Sijue tugged her hoodie tighter as she navigated puddles and gutters. A volumetric ad flickered to life as she passed the Jade Lotus bar—its hologram hovering like a disconnected dream from another dimension. It promised drinks with cognitive enhancers for premium customers. The image briefly glitched as rain sliced through its light field.

Lin didn't break stride. The air tasted of wet asphalt, mold, and something else—a fetid exhalation from the city's drains. In this liminal hour, Shanghai's digital mask flickered with data exhaustion. Secrets seeped out like invisible odors, enjoying their brief moment of freedom before melding into the night.

She slipped through back alleys, her steps slapping on wet pavement, while her hoodie's IR mesh pulsed with random heat blooms, ghosting her outline. Smart-pavement twitched under her boots, piezoelectric sensors stuttering with static, their data ending in rat-eaten wires. Her frame—honed by MMA and three years in the Korean National Police—moved with practiced stealth; shoulders low, elbows tucked in, every motion economical.

She doubled back twice, her senses taut for pursuit: the distant slap of a footfall, the faint whirr of drone rotors fading in and out as they hovered high above. They couldn't flag her; her air-gapped smart-contacts spoofed handshake protocols, the trade-off a minor jitter in her tactical overlay. She dismissed it with a couple of blinks and kept her rhythm.

A drunken businessman lurched past, breath reeking

of *baijiu* and synthetic stimulants. Lin sidestepped with a fighter's precision, her hand brushing the ceramic blade at her hip, an old-school weapon she trusted like a friend. Commander Crane's voice echoed in her mind: Emotions are malware. Uninstall them. Now a familiar refrain, the warmth collapsing into mission logic, tenderness overwritten by the report.

She'd believed it once—*before* Peter.

The alley behind Lujiazui Tower formed a rare dead zone in the city's smart-grid—a pocket of interference where graffiti bloomed unchecked and refuse piled against crumbling brickwork, still scarred by old flood lines. Lin slipped through a basement entrance of an abandoned dumpling shop, the air thick with the aroma of soup broth and fried oil. She crossed quickly, boots squelching on cracked tiles long neglected. The rear exit opened onto a passage the city's AI trackers had deprecated—one of three blind spots she'd memorized from countless family visits.

Her destination loomed ahead: an old capsule hotel, its faded sign a relic in a high-tech world, neon tubes sputtering half-lit characters in forgotten fonts. The building leaned, concrete stained with rust veins from leaking rebar. Rusted IoT sensors long silent studded its façade, their plastic housings cracked like insect carapaces. Russian Doll's intel had flagged it as "sub-threshold infrastructure"—too obsolete to monitor, its power draw too low to register on the city's adaptive surveillance heuristics.

Her breathing quickened—not out of fear, but from rising anticipation. Russian Doll's protocols were clear: emotional attachments compromised effectiveness, creating vulnerabilities. What she was about to do violated every rule. But after Crane's encrypted message three hours earlier—*Return to Lazarus without delay*—this might be her last chance. If he discovered this breach, suspension would be the merciful option.

The lobby was a 2020s time capsule, with fake wood paneling warped from dampness, burnt-orange carpet pockmarked with cigarette burns from a pre-ban era. Vending machines hummed faintly, dispensing knockoff energy gels in crinkling foil. She climbed a set of narrow stairs, her footsteps muffled by the sensor-free carpet. There would be no data trail, just threads fraying under her soles.

The hallway stretched like a snake's throat, lined with circular capsule doors stacked three high. Dented aluminum hatches, some sealed with magnetic locks, fused shut. A flickering fluorescent light cast jagged shadows, buzzing erratically in the humidity.

The second pod on the left hung slightly ajar, a sliver of darkness within. Lin paused, listening to the building's groans—pipes contracting in the cold, rain drumming on a tin awning—then ducked inside, pulling the hatch closed with a soft magnetic click.

Peter Harrington was waiting inside, his Navy SEAL frame folded tight. Six feet of disciplined muscle strained against curved walls, knees drawn up to fit the capsule's coffin-like confines. Dark-rimmed eyes burned bright in a stubbled face, shadows carving hollows under cheekbones. His fingers lingered over a battered Rolex, a GMT-Master II, inherited from his father, now lost to dementia, its mechanical heartbeat defying a digital world, its second hand sweeping with analog defiance.

Lin didn't waste a second. She straddled him, the curved wall biting her spine, belt buckle cold against her stomach. Three-day stubble scraped her chin like sandpaper. It felt even better when he buried his face in her sex. They fucked like every rule they'd ever swallowed just turned to ash. Russian Doll demanded they be weapons, emotions purged by Commander Crane's conditioning, but here, they could believe it was a world of their making, even if only for a fleeting heartbeat.

When they parted, breathless, the stale air thickened with their mingled scents. They lay tangled, but the comfort was fleeting. Lin's 24-hour compassionate leave was shrinking, and Peter's unsanctioned detour to Shanghai had burned his margin for error.

Lin's voice was soft but urgent, her cadence tinged with Korean: "I wasn't sure my signal got through. When I saw Crane's recall order—"

"I got it." Peter's chest rose and fell beneath her touch, but the SEAL was already reasserting control—pulse steadying under her fingers. "Can't believe you managed to arrange this palatial abode without Crane's knowledge."

"Good things come in small packages."

Peter acknowledged her, squeezing gently. "Crane thinks my transport from Taipei is delayed for maintenance. I've got maybe ten hours before he realizes I'm not in Bangkok." He was about to continue saying something, but he broke off, his voice momentarily choking.

"What, what is it?"

With effort, he collected himself. "Tapei was a disaster ..."

Lin shifted, her KNP instincts taking over. "What happened?"

Peter propped himself on an elbow, his fingers worrying on the bezel of his watch. "Crane sent me and Clay to stop a Chinese agent codenamed Finger at LinkAxon in Hsinchu Science Park. Neurotech facility, locked tight, retinal gates, EMP-hardened doors. Orders came with only twenty minutes' notice. No briefing, no prep."

Lin's brow furrowed. "That's breaking protocol. Even emergency intercepts get a threat assessment."

"Yeah. Clay showed up like they'd pulled him from another op. His eyes were bloodshot, his shirt was soaked with sweat."

"Nervous?"

"No, this was …" His eyes grew distant, searching for words that could convey what he hadn't fully grasped. "Crane said it was now or never. Finger was moving that night. I didn't argue," he said, gesturing with his hands. "Clay and I went way back—Budapest, Istanbul, Berlin. I thought I knew him. But in Taipei … something was off."

"Off how?" Lin pressed.

Peter's gaze drifted, replaying the memory. "He was faster. His reflexes were sharper than any operative I've trained with. And aggressive too, like he was itching for contact." He shook his head like he still didn't believe it. "He kept dropping tech terms like 'neural architecture,' 'quantum encryption,' stuff you'd hear from a lab geek, not Clay."

"Inside knowledge?"

Peter shrugged. "Maybe. We cornered Finger in a server room. The data gates were air-gapped, so remote hacks weren't possible. Even quantum decryption would have taken hours. Finger knew it. When we got there, he was already prying a cryogenic drive module from one of the racks—a fist-sized slab humming with superconducting coils, matte-black, but already frosting with blooms of liquid helium coolant. I estimated one physical unit must have held petabytes of data. He was about to stuff it in a Faraday case." Peter's jaw clenched. "Then Clay froze. Just … locked up. Started muttering, 'Istanbul … not Taipei.'

His pupils were unevenly dilated. I yelled at him to snap out of it, but he called out the Istanbul mission codes—'Alpha Seven, Delta Nine'—like he was reliving it. Gave our position away."

Lin sat up slightly, the movement constrained by the capsule's curve. "That doesn't make sense."

"Yeah, you tell me," Peter said. He paused, ran a hand through his hair, the motion jerky, agitated. "Because Finger dropped him dead with a clean headshot. Single bullet." Peter's voice trembled with emotion. "I tried to stop the bleeding. That's when I saw it—a fresh scar behind his left ear. Surgical. Recent." He met her eyes. "We shared a safehouse in Odessa, after Istanbul, six months ago. It wasn't there then."

Lin thought about her mother, her fingers moving to the base of her own skull, unconsciously checking. Neural augmentation. The whispers from her biotech lectures suddenly felt less theoretical. "Maybe it was medical. Tumor removal?"

"That's what I thought." Peter said, dropping to barely a whisper. "But after I carried him to our rendezvous, a van pulled up. Masked men, no insignia. They quoted our codeword—'White Rhino'—so I handed him over. But, Lin …" He shook his head. "It felt wrong. As soon as they realized he was dead, they lost their precision. Up until that moment, they had operated like clockwork, but it was like someone had thrown sand into the gears. I'd call it panic, but they were too professional for that. They covered it up by throwing him into the van, like garbage collectors, then sped off."

Lin stared, her mind racing. The capsule's walls seemed to press inward. "It doesn't sound like they were ours."

"I don't know who they were. But something's wrong, and it's not me." Peter rubbed his temples, then half-laughed. "Crane's going to blame me. I can feel it already. I might as well hand in my resignation right now. Rob him of the chance to scapegoat me."

"That's a bit excessive, don't you think?"

"Not at all. I'm the only independent witness. What do you think that means?"

Lin considered. "Okay, so if Clay wasn't Clay, who was he?"

"That's the million-dollar question, isn't it?"

"But you've thought about it?"

"All the way from Taipei."

"And?"

Peter's fingers stilled on his watch. "I've heard the rumors ... in the mess hall, in the corridors ... neural augmentation, Crane's not satisfied with ordinary human intelligence." He met her gaze. "What if they're experimenting with us?"

Lin shrunk from the possibility, the hairs on her neck rising. "That's illegal. UN conventions—"

"Since when has that stopped people like Crane?" Peter's voice became more strident. "Think about it. The scar, the reflexes, Clay acting like someone uploaded combat protocols into a body that knew the moves but not the mission." He leaned forward. The capsule creaked under his weight. "What if he's a prototype? They thought he was mission ready except he wasn't?"

Lin wanted to reject the idea outright. It sounded like science fiction horror. Monstrous. But her training—the endless simulations, the conditioning, Crane's cold assessments—suddenly took on a different cast. The scar behind Clay's ear, the off-script behavior of the extraction team … "You think Crane—"

"I think someone at Russian Doll is running an off-books program," Peter said. "And I'm the witness who wasn't supposed to survive Taipei."

Lin let that sink in, the implications spreading through her like ice crystals. She became aware of her own heartbeat, loud in the silence between them. "If that's true, then we're in this way over our heads."

"Which is why maybe now's the time to get out. Or blow it open …"

Lin shook her head. "Peter, you're just one man."

Peter huffed.

"I think," Lin said carefully, "if what you're saying is true—even if it's just a grain of truth—we need to protect ourselves. From each other."

It was an idea Peter could agree with. "Like something they don't know about us. Can never know."

"Yeah," Lin said, certain now. "Like a secret handshake—or a code ..."

"Passwords," Peter said simply. "But not just any passwords."

"Exactly. Something before Russian Doll. Before Crane. A memory so personal, so specific, they couldn't fake it because they don't know it exists." She met his eyes. "Something from childhood. Sensory. Emotional. The kind of thing that lives in your bones, not in any file."

Peter searched his past. Ran a hand through his short-cropped hair. "When I was twelve, I snuck into my dad's library late one night. He had a first edition of *The Count of Monte Cristo*. It had this cinnamon-colored cloth cover. Smelled like old paper and dust. It was his pride and joy." A faint smile touched his lips. "I read it under a quilt with a crappy LED flashlight. Felt like I was stealing something sacred. Dad caught me, grounded me for a month ... but I didn't care. I'd fallen in love with the story, with justice served cold." He looked at Lin. "That smell, the scratchy feel of that cloth, the fear and thrill of getting caught—that's mine. That's Peter Harrington, not Agent Six."

Lin watched him, feeling the umbilical cord of truth grow between them. "Seoul," she whispered. "A summer thunderstorm killed the city's grid. Everything went dark. Smart-buildings, digital signs, traffic lights—total black-out." She closed her eyes. "I snuck out while my parents were frantic. Went to an old temple in Bukhansan. Rain was sheeting off the tiled roof, lightning cracked, flash-bulbing the shadows into day." Her voice softened. "For a split second, the courtyard lit up ... and I saw my grandmother by the altar, looking peaceful. It didn't scare me. It felt right, like I was part of something that the physical world couldn't reach." She opened her eyes. "I can still smell the wet stone, the incense, and feel the cold rain. It's a moment trapped in time, an impossible stillness. It's part of me now. Who I am."

Peter reached out, fingers brushing hers. "So if I ever need to know it's really you, I ask for that moment?"

"Ask for Temple Storm," Lin said.

"And if you need to know it's me?"

"You'll tell me about Monte Cristo."

Peter studied her face in the dim ambience. "Temple Storm," he said quietly.

Lin closed her eyes, "Yes, that's me."

"Monte Cristo," he said. "Cinnamon and dust. My father's disappointment. Worth every minute." His mouth quirked. "That's me, always has been."

The weight of their pact hung in the air. Lin's voice softened, seeking something normal. "You ever miss it? Before all this?"

Peter leaned back, a genuine smile forming. "Yeah. Summers at my uncle's cabin in Montana. No smart-tech, no grid. Just pine trees and a frozen lake. I'd fish with a battered bamboo rod. Catch nothing but sunburn." He chuckled softly. "The world felt honest, you know?" He looked at her. "Can you imagine? A copy of me would be an abomination. An affront to Nature."

"There's only room for one of you here anyway," Lin said, lips quirking into a rare smile.

Peter laughed softly. "What about you?"

Lin brushed a strand of hair from her eyes. "Shanghai, before it got so wired. My grandmother's tiny kitchen. The smell of her spicy noodles—always too much chili, burning your nose before you even took a bite. She'd tell stories about neighbors who helped without contracts, trust that didn't need biometric scans." A wistful sigh escaped her. "I'd kill for one bowl right now."

Peter chuckled. "Knowing her, they'd probably melt my tongue off. You'd have me crying, SEAL training wouldn't even save me from that!"

"Oh, absolutely. She didn't believe in 'mild.'"

They shared a quiet laugh, a fragile bridge to something human. Peter's eyes grew heavy, the adrenaline crash hitting hard. "God, I'm beat," he murmured. "Haven't slept right since Taipei."

"Rest," Lin said softly, her hand covering his. "I'm here."

Peter's head tilted back, breathing slowing. Within moments, the tension in his frame ebbed, and he was asleep, face soft with unguarded peace.

Lin sat in the humming quiet, alone with his sleeping form. Her fingers found the brass prayer wheel beneath her hoodie, its metal warm against her skin, worn smooth by her grandmother's hands, etched with mantras whispering under her thumb. She spun it slowly, its ratchet sound a comforting familiarity. "The wheel turns for everyone," her grandmother's voice echoed. "What we send out returns, magnified."

She thought of Clay. The implications of tampering, of losing control. Those thoughts made her shudder with revulsion. Being herself, having control over her authenticity, meant everything. Despite her commitment to serve her country, to offer herself as a sacrifice if necessary, what mattered most to her was choice. If she was going to do that, it had to be on her conscience, not Crane's. The situation with Clay suggested otherwise.

Her prayer wheel stopped and clicked into place.

The cosmos had turned, its fate waiting to be written.

– 2 –

Suspension

Russian Doll Administrative Wing, Platform Lazarus, Gulf of Thailand

THE ELEVATOR climbed through Platform Lazarus's steel spine with mechanical precision, each floor marked by a soft chime echoing in the cramped compartment. Peter Harrington stared at the scuffed aluminum wall, his reflection blurring like a pointillist painting. The ascent from the submarine bay felt endless—forty-seven floors from the platform's waterline to the administrative levels where careers lived and died behind soundproof doors.

Agent Martinez sidled up to him, his hand resting near his sidearm with the practiced ease of someone who'd escorted one too many failed operatives to the scrap heap. His olive complexion bore the weathered look of a fieldworker, but his eyes held the flat wariness of internal security. "First time up from the deep docks?" he asked, his tone forced, like he was reading from a script.

Peter's jaw tightened. The question stung, implying he was a rookie lost in the platform's maze, when in fact he was their most senior operative, memorized every corridor, exit, and chokepoint during training seven years ago. "I know my way around," he said, his voice edged with the irritation of a man tired of being underestimated.

Martinez shrugged, unfazed. "Just trying to break the ice. You look like you could use a friend."

The elevator shuddered as it passed the platform's center of gravity, that precise point where the 150-meter-long structure balanced against the ocean's endless pull. Peter's stomach lurched—not from the motion, but from the weight of what waited above. He'd been summoned, not invited, and his SEAL training screamed warnings about the difference.

The doors whispered open at the forty-second floor, revealing a corridor stretching like an artery through the platform's administrative heart. Battered sheet-steel panels lined the walls, plastered with fire safety and evacuation posters. The air tasted of evaporated oil and industrial cleaners, and seeped into everything, including every pore of the skin, earning it the nickname: "the bilge."

Peter stepped out with deliberate confidence, but it was forced and he knew it. He chastised himself to relax, take what comes. Martinez fell into step, keeping the regulation three-foot gap demanded for escorts. Their bodies moved in sync across the boot-marked floor, a behavior that harked back to their shared military experience.

"You don't need to shadow me," Peter said, irritation slipping through. The words sounded muffled, swallowed by acoustic dampening that made conversation feel stifled.

Martinez's smile lacked warmth. "Orders, Harrington. From the big dog himself."

"Didn't realize I was that important. Which must make you what? His bone?"

Martinez's hand twitched toward his sidearm—then stilled. His stiff glance carried a warning.

They passed offices where analysts worked behind soundproof glass, their faces bathed in the blue glow of classified displays. Some glanced up, their eyes flickering with curiosity or pity. Word spread fast in tight quarters: Peter's failure in Taipei was on everyone's lips. Peter stoically kept his chin up, he didn't want to give anyone the pleasure of his humiliation. It was unbecoming of a soldier.

The corridor branched at a junction marked by a holographic directory cycling through languages—English, Russian, Mandarin, Arabic—reflecting Russian Doll's global reach. "Left here," Martinez said, though Peter was already turning, his familiarity a small defiance.

Morgan Crane's office sat at the corridor's end, its reinforced door bearing a nameplate and a biometric scanner that glowed red. Peter approached, each step a countdown. He'd rehearsed this during the elevator ride, mapping responses and contingencies with SEAL precision.

Martinez leaned against the opposite wall, his posture alert but relaxed. "Good luck," he said, perfectly inflected without the least conviction.

Peter didn't even bother acknowledging him and knocked twice on the brushed steel door, the sound coming back like the deadened toll of a cast-iron bell. Silence stretched, long enough to feel like Crane was playing power games, making him wait to underscore the stature of their ranks.

The door opened with a heavy clank, like a prison cell, and Peter's eyes settled on Crane standing behind his stainless steel desk. Worn fatigues hung on his craggy frame—a tired executioner who'd dispensed with ceremony long ago.

Beyond the reinforced glass that provided sweeping views of the outside world, the Gulf of Thailand simmered. The late afternoon sun, hammered flat by thick humidity, glinted off swells that slapped against the platform's massive pylons. The air in the office was cool and recycled, a stark contrast to the tropical heat haze outside, where the first bruise-colored clouds of a coming squall were gathering on the horizon.

Peter stood rigid before Crane's desk, SEAL training keeping his posture parade-ground straight despite the fury in his veins. The desk was cluttered with encrypted tablets flickering with mission reports and personnel files. A faded photo sat amid the chaos—Crane's son in a Navy uniform, his smile frozen before a mine in the Kaesong Corridor turned him into a memory.

Holographic displays flickered behind Crane, their blue-white glow casting shadows across walls lined with commendations from governments that denied Russian Doll's existence. The largest showed Taipei footage, bleached under UV lighting, stark as an X-ray.

Crane gestured at the display, his voice flat, commanding. "I've studied the footage. What went wrong?"

"Good day to you too, Sir."

Crane ignored Peter's salutation. He returned his gaze to the display. The camera held steady, showing Harrington and Clay moving through LinkAxon's Hsinchu corridors with tactical grace. The UV stripped color, reducing them to ghostly figures. Every detail stood out—hand signals, pauses, head turns ...

"Here," Crane said, pausing the feed. Sebastian Clay was frozen, mid-step, his head tilted as if lost. Peter's mouth moved, the audio silent. "What did you say to him?"

"I told him to move."

"But he locked up."

"He said something about Istanbul … not Taipei. He went off-script, like his mind hiccuped. That's when Finger took the shot."

The next frame showed the headshot, blood spreading on concrete in patterns too precise for art, too final for fiction. Peter's chest tightened, the scar behind Clay's ear burning in his mind.

Crane killed the display, banishing Clay's death to digital limbo. His gray eyes, sharp as frost, carried three decades of intelligence work. "Your job was simple—stop Finger from stealing the data. You failed."

Peter bristled. "I'd have stopped him if you hadn't sent an impostor."

The words crackled in the recycled air. The office fell silent, save for the distant thrum of the platform's engines.

A look of disgust passed across Crane's weathered features. "Are you suggesting that I set you up?"

Peter's voice hardened. "I saw a fresh scar behind his left ear. It wasn't there in Istanbul. You tell me."

Crane leaned forward, his tone probing. "You used the word, 'impostor.' What are you really thinking?"

Peter hesitated. He wasn't sure if this was a test or not. "I don't believe Seb had any reason to have that scar. Which means he must have been tampered with. That and the fact that he wasn't himself."

Crane's composure flickered, a micro-expression of concern too quick for most to catch, but Peter's training spotted it. Then a sardonic grin spread. "A scar and a theory. You're reaching."

"Am I? You saw the video. Seb wasn't himself. He knew the layout like he had it tattooed on his brain. But I never saw him at training. You dumped him on me like a ghost. Why?"

"You want to know?"

"Yeah I want to know. I'm sick and tired—"

"We cloned him."

Peter's jaw dropped. The words hung in the recycled air, impossible. "You ... cloned him?"

"A fully mature copy. Conditioned and trained."

Peter's mind reeled, scrambling to fit the pieces into place—the scar, the reflexes, the off-script behavior. The horrifying truth snapped into focus. "But not trained well enough," he said, daring to criticize.

Crane tossed his head sideways, as if discarding the comment. "He served his purpose."

"Which was?"

"To save your life."

Peter stared at Crane like he was speaking a foreign language. "To save my life?"

"It wasn't Finger who took the shot."

Now Peter was really thrown.

"We got some last minute intel. They had a sniper. We didn't know where, or when, all we knew was that someone was going to get hurt."

"So it could have been me?"

"It could have."

Peter was stunned.

"The odds were 50-50, but I think I stacked them in your favor by sending in Clay."

"As a decoy?"

Crane's expression remained impassive. "I've already told you more than you should know," he said, and walked over to the windows and gazed at the view outside. "We're in a dirty game, Harrington. Sometimes we have to fight fire with fire. But one thing I can tell you. If you so much as open your mouth about this to anyone, and I mean *anyone*, I won't be able to help you. Do you understand?"

Peter opened his mouth to protest, but Crane stopped him.

"There are bigger forces at play here than just the two of us. You got it?"

"What kind of forces? You want to enlighten me?"

"No."

Peter swallowed hard. "So what happens next?"

Crane swiped a hand across his desk. "What happens next? I'm standing you down. You're too close to this."

Peter blinked, the words hitting him like shrapnel.

Crane's tone shifted. "Your identity has been compromised. That means revoking your clearance—temporarily."

Peter bristled defensively. "You're sidelining me."

"A medical leave," Crane corrected. "Take a break, clear your head."

"My head's clear," Peter snapped.

Crane pressed the intercom. Justine Fairweather appeared, her charcoal suit crisp, and placed a data tablet before Peter. "Sign here, here, and here."

Peter's eyes locked on Crane, fury and helplessness clashing. He hesitated.

Crane sighed. "Refuse, and your insurance and superannuation freeze. You know how this works."

Peter stiffened, rage surging. He forced his hands to unclench, his voice calm but brittle. "Of course. I'd expect nothing less." He took the stylus and signed, each stroke an unwilling surrender.

Crane gestured to the door, dismissive, final.

As Peter's footsteps faded down the corridor, Crane stood motionless at the window, watching storm clouds mass on the horizon. The Gulf churned, indifferent to human secrets.

He slammed a fist on his desk. The photo of his son slid an inch, the boy's smile now crooked. "Damn it, Justine. I just sidelined Harrington. We need a replacement, fast!"

Justine gazed at him with weary sympathy. "I have a suggestion, but you won't like it."

"Try me."

"Lin Sijue."

"She's still a cadet."

"Yes. But hear me out." Fairweather opened a paper folder and slid two photos across the desk. "Which one do you think is Sijue?"

Crane looked them over and grumbled, "I've got about as much chance as tossing a coin." He tapped the photo on the right.

"That's Kang Hyuk's dead sister."

Crane's face transformed with understanding. "Clever. But Lazarus won't be happy if he finds out we're going over his head."

Fairweather didn't blink. "Sometimes algorithms are too predictable."

Crane looked at her dubiously. "You're asking me to bet against the machine's psychometric profile?"

"The machine lost us Clay," Fairweather countered, her voice low. "It can't measure defiance. Or love."

Crane held her gaze for a long moment. His face was briefly thrown into stark contrast as a lightning bolt shattered the sky. "Damn it. Start the paperwork."

"My pleasure."

– 3 –

The Assignment

Russian Doll Headquarters,
Platform Lazarus, Gulf of Thailand

THE TRAINING arena, forty feet above Platform Lazarus's waterline, was a claustrophobic box of battered metal sheeting, its dents and rust scars etched by decades of saltwater corrosion. Grimy 40-watt bulbs cast wan yellow light, dimming when the generators stuttered under load. The notorious scent of "the bilge" mingled with occasional whiffs of welding smoke from patchwork repairs.

The rising waves outside could be heard crashing against the rig's 50-tonne pylon legs, each collision sending a muffled whoomp reverberating through the steel framework, as if a giant was hammering them from the outside.

Lin Sijue paced the octagonal mat, its rubber surface scuffed and splitting from years of boots and falls, her navy tactical gear clinging like a second skin. Racks along the walls held MMA gear—bamboo *kendo* sticks, chipped *shinai*, and cracked sparring pads, their leather reeking of mildew and sweat, stacked beside rusted dumbbells.

Her opponent, Brad Lee, Russian Doll's MMA trainer, stood opposite, his compact frame taut with the coiled menace of Hong Kong's underground fight dens. His shaved head caught the dim light like scoured granite, dark eyes weighing her with respect and challenge. "Ready, Sijue?" he asked, his voice steady and focused.

Lin nodded, her breath even, her Seoul police training meshing with Russian Doll's lethal curriculum. She lunged, snapping a crisp jab toward Brad's shoulder, expecting a defensive sidestep. But Brad was a squall breaking loose. He countered with blistering speed, grabbing her arm and slamming her to the mat with a whack that rang off the metal walls. The impact stole her breath, leaving her dazed and gasping on the mat. Brad pounced, locking her in a chokehold to add salt to the wound, his grip a steel trap that dimmed her vision like oil slicking over glass.

He released her, stepping back as she staggered to her knees, sucking air. "What'd you do wrong?" he asked, his tone sharp, dissecting her error.

Lin braced herself on the mat, hands flat, her mind replaying the brutal clash. "I thought you'd block," she admitted, voice tight with self-reproach.

"Wrong," Brad said, circling her like a hawk eyeing a stumble. "It's not your hands, Sijue. It's your head. You attacked assuming I'd defend. I hit your move, outran your plan with speed and power. In a real fight, you strike as they strike—ride their force, not your guess."

Lin nodded, the lesson striking deep, a flare in her fog of exhaustion. Brad's words echoed her grandmother's teachings—karma as a cycle of action and consequence, not miscalculation. She stored the insight, her resolve hardening like steel tempered in the ocean's chill. The mat, scarred with years of sweat and struggle, felt like a temple floor, her training a ritual to balance fate's wheel.

Lin headed to the showers, a cramped stall of rusted panels and creaking pipes, where tepid water sputtered from a corroded nozzle, washing away sweat and the rig's oily residue. She dried off with a threadbare towel, its rough weave abrading her skin, the faint sandalwood scent of her grandmother's prayer wheel lingering in her mind as she dressed in fresh tactical gear. Her damp hair clung to her neck as she moved toward the water distillery plant, their prearranged blind spot.

To reach it, Lin navigated a treacherous catwalk of exposed steel beams that were slick with moisture and grease dropped from years of maintenance. 60 meters below, the ocean roiled, the storm now shifting into full swing. Maintenance workers battening down hatches were too busy to notice her silhouette as it leaped from beam to beam, her movements timed to security cameras' blind sweeps, fingers finding purchase on rust-bitten manifolds and slimed pipes.

She reached a vertical H-beam and, clinging to it, scaled upward, muscles burning as she hauled herself onto the water distillery platform. She landed on a grated deck strewn with rusted bolts and pipe couplings. The distillery's churn—pumps chugging seawater through filters—signaled she had reached her safe haven. She dropped her bag onto the deck and waited.

In a sterile lab three floors above, Dr. Avery Quinn and Dr. Elana Raskova stood over Sebastian Clay's autopsy table, the air sharp with antiseptic and blood. Seb's body lay under harsh LED light, his skull a mangled ruin, cortical tissue splayed like a broken puzzle.

Quinn extracted a graphene electrode from the temporal cortex, his gloved hands trembling as he placed it under the microscope. The fibrils appeared immediately—amyloid-like tangles clogging the lattice.

"Five kilo-ohms," he said flatly.

Raskova leaned in, her jaw tight. "Impossible. My edits were clean."

"Then explain these." Quinn gestured at the microscope.

She studied the fibrils, her pale eyes narrowing. "Contamination. Your sterilization protocol—"

"Was standard. 134 degrees. Logged." Quinn pulled back the skull flap, exposing the bullet's devastation. "The fibrils tanked his decision loop. That's why we lost LinkAxon."

"Or your lattice placement was off," Raskova countered. "Point-two millimeters triggers astrocyte overactivation."

"My placement was verified."

"In this rust bucket?" She gestured at the lab's grimy corners, her Moscow accent sharp with contempt.

Quinn's voice rose. "A second-gen implant failed and we just handed Black Hand a strategic advantage. We're not debugging—we're containing a catastrophe."

"Calm down Quinn. You're getting on my nerves!"

Quinn gave her a goofy look. "You keep trying to blame my surgical technique, when we both know your gene edits are the weak link."

Raskova's fist clenched, latex squeaking. "My CRISPR edits were triple-verified."

"But not your reagents."

"We told Crane we needed more time!" Her voice cracked with frustration. "He's expecting a marathon when we haven't learned to walk."

"You're the one who promised him results."

"Because we can do it!" She wiped her hands on her lab

coat, forcing composure. "Harrington's next. He should be our priority."

Quinn hesitated, doubt clouding his face. "His implant's 93 percent stable. Higher than Clay. But—"

"But what?"

"I don't know. Something's off."

"You're overthinking."

"Am I?"

A heavy silence fell between them, broken only by the hum of the lab's refrigeration units. Then—Crane's voice crackled through the comms. "I've authorized Harrington's activation. What his status?"

Quinn glanced at Raskova. "Conditioning's almost complete. Running final tests this week."

"Excellent. Keep me updated."

The comms died.

Quinn gave Raskova a wan smile. She shrugged, but neither could look away from Clay's ruined body.

They both knew this wouldn't be the last time.

In the water distillery plant, a cavernous chamber of hissing pipes and churning pumps, Peter Harrington waited in a blind spot where cameras failed, their lenses fogged by steam and grease. The space reeked of hydraulic fluid and rust, lit by a string of incandescent bulbs, their grime-streaked glass battling against the gloom. Peter had bribed a maintenance worker—Torres, a grizzled hand in grease-stained overalls—with a wad of cash to slip through a maintenance hatch, its rusted hinges groaning under corrosion. His revoked clearance left no other way in, his suspension order effective but a small grace period to collect his personal effects left him time. His fingers tightened on his vintage Rolex, its ticking a metronome counting down to exile.

Lin slipped into the blind spot, her acrobatic traverse complete, her tactical gear fresh but her hair still damp from the shower, carrying the faint scent of soap over the rig's oily stain. Her competence—her deadly beauty—tightened Peter's chest with emotions Russian Doll couldn't erase.

Their kiss was desperate, hungry, heavy with longing and the fear each meeting might be their last. Her lips tasted of soap and sweat, his of suspension's bitter odor. For a fleeting moment, they were just two people, not operatives weighing freedom's risks.

Peter pulled back, his voice low, urgent, shielded by the distillery's steam and noise. "I've been suspended. No clearance, no access—'medical leave' pending investigation. I'm heading back to Idaho."

Lin's eyes saddened. "Idaho? So we'll … see less of each other?"

Peter nodded, the weight of it crushing. "Yeah. Less time, more distance. Crane's orders. You must be nearly mission ready."

Lin shook her head, doubt crossing her features. "Not sure. There's hints about a briefing."

"Tread carefully," Peter warned, his hands finding hers, tracing calluses from weapons and martial arts. "I don't trust Crane. He's playing a deeper game. He told me as much—"

"About Clay?"

"He admitted that Clay may have been tampered with."

Lin's eyes widened.

"So you were right?"

"Yeah, but it goes deeper. How deep ... I don't know. I've been locked out."

Lin stared at him, didn't dare to say what they both thought.

"Listen," Peter said, "whether it was us or someone else, it's a lead. The cloning cat's out of the bag. We're in an arms race now—except the bullets are no longer metal, but human flesh."

Lin shuddered.

Peter squeezed her hand, whispering close. "Remember our code words."

Lin nodded, their pact a lifeline.

"Contact me when you know your mission," Peter urged. "Back channels—dead drops, encrypted bursts, off their grid."

"Will do," Lin said, preparing herself for the inevitable separation.

Their parting was wordless, heavy with trust over training, connection over loyalty. Lin slipped out, retracing her acrobatic path along the beams, leaving Peter with the steady bulb and his father's watch. The distillery's hum normalized, and they resumed their roles—Lin prepping for Crane's mission, Peter navigating suspension's limbo, probing for truth. Neither spoke of love, but their ember burned against conditioning.

The wheel of karma turned, gaining momentum with each choice, each line crossed. In Platform Lazarus's depths, surrounded by the ocean's ceaseless battering, their decisions rippled outward, unseen. Above, Quinn and Raskova wrestled with their protocols, while Crane studied mission parameters testing Lin beyond combat. The chessboard shifted, each move a gamble on identity itself.

In the distillery, their reunion's scent lingered like incense at an altar to hope, in a world that forgot what human connection meant.

– 4 –

Briefing

Russian Doll Headquarters,
Platform Lazarus, Gulf of Thailand

LIN SIJUE stepped into Morgan Crane's office, the door shutting with a heavy clank. Crane stood by the blast-proof window, his silhouette sharp against the squall as its fury lashed the rig's superstructure. Below, the swells of the Gulf of Thailand had grown to their full height, their force now sufficient to shudder the floor beneath their feet.

Lin's adrenaline surged, Peter's warning from their clandestine meeting echoing: *Crane's playing a deeper game.* She schooled her expression, burying the memory of Peter's urgent whisper, their desperate kiss in the distillery pushed out of consciousness. Alone with Crane for the first time since Taipei's fallout, she searched his reflection for clues—some tell of the hidden agenda Peter feared.

Crane's face, half-lit by the ocean's roil, was a map of hard lines and suppressed shadows. His gray eyes, sharp as frost, shifted toward her, but they held a distant ache, as if the sea's fury mirrored an inner storm. She noticed the framed color photograph of the young man on his desk, had heard the rumous that it was his dead son, but she avoided lingering her gaze on it too long. She didn't want to pretend sympathy for an emotional history she knew little about.

Crane turned, his voice rough with the grit of decades spent issuing orders that left blood on foreign soil. "How's the body feeling after your jaunt with Brad Lee?"

"I won't make the same mistakes again."

Crane smiled knowingly. "There's always new mistakes to make."

"What am I here for, sir?"

A pause, his gaze drifting to the photograph, heavy with unspoken weight. "He could thread a needle at three hundred meters. Best in the business." His eyes locked onto hers, probing for a reaction. "But perfect shots don't mean a damn thing if you hesitate when it counts. Out there, your enemy's not just shooting back—you're up against their mind, their will. Sometimes, you have to look them in the eye."

Lin stood motionless, her silence a shield honed in childhood temples where stillness spoke louder than words. She drew strength from her prayer wheel, currently in her personal locker, silent. She offered no nod, no pride—just a steady gaze that refused to yield.

Crane's eyes narrowed slightly, as if her restraint posed an interesting equation. He moved to his workstation, swiped his security card and pushed a video file to his monitor. He pressed play: a man's face materialized—high cheekbones carved by violence, black-ice eyes, a cruel smirk promising pain. A subtle irregularity in his gait flickered in one frame, a faint asymmetry quickly corrected, hinting at some concealed injury.

"This is Kang Hyuk." Crane spoke with the gravity of someone who'd studied monsters. "Forty-one years old, though he's lived twice that in violence. Bok Yeong's right hand, but calling him an enforcer undersells the man. Kang doesn't just follow orders—he shapes them. When Black Hand needs something impossible done, they send him."

The video shifted: Kang in Pyongyang's bunkers, executing defectors with a pistol's cold precision; in Macau's casinos, moving through crowds with a predator's grace; in Seoul's rain-slick alleys, slipping past cameras like a phantom. Each frame seeped with lethality—a man who thrived in chaos's embrace.

Crane continued, his voice taking on the measured cadence of someone recounting intelligence gathered over years. "Kang's story begins with hunger—real starvation, not metaphor, in Hamhung's frozen streets. U.S. sanctions in the 2010s were meant to squeeze Pyongyang's elite, but pressure always trickles down until it chokes the marrow. His mother died from untreated pneumonia. His brother disappeared on a train and never returned. By 2019, he was the last one breathing. He doesn't just blame America—he sees it as a virus, a slow hemorrhage that bled his family dry. That kind of hatred doesn't fade. It ferments. Crystallizes into something precise and unrelenting."

"Spetsnaz doctrine trained him. Electro-pads—reflex accelerators, subdermal shock buffers, sub-clinical doses of amphetamines. His confirmed kill count breaks seventy, but numbers lie. He kills for function, not pleasure—except when it serves a message. There are anomalies in his file: sparing a defector's daughter, honoring a fallen rival with burial rites. Moments of mercy, or psychological warfare? Either way, he doesn't fit the mold. He thrives in ambiguity. That's what makes him difficult to predict."

The video froze on Kang's smirk, his eyes seeming to drill into Lin's. "Apart from his pride, he has one weakness." Crane paused, drawing out the moment. Then he flipped another image onto the monitor. "This is Yeon-Hee."

Lin's eyes widened at the photo.

"Recognize any resemblance?" Crane asked. It was clearly rhetorical. "Other agencies would kill for this face. You're our jackpot."

"So you want me to impersonate her?" Lin asked tentatively.

"Yes and no," Crane explained. "She died when Kang was a teenager."

"Oh ..."

"But a chance to see a loved one again—what man wouldn't move heaven and earth for that?"

"I understand."

"I don't think you do," Crane said, his voice shifting to something colder, more surgical. He let his gaze drift— slow, deliberate—over the line of her shoulders, the taper of her waist, the swell beneath the fabric of her shirt. Not lust. Inventory. "You're counting on the usual tricks, aren't you? The tilt of the hip, the half-smile, the little pause before you speak. The things that make most men trip over their own tongues."

Lin's chin lifted, defiant, not out of conscious awareness, but an uncontrolled reflex.

Crane pressed harder. "Kang doesn't negotiate with bait. He takes it, uses it, discards it. Your confidence? It's a costume he'll strip off before you realize the game's already over. You'll think you're steering; he'll have you pinned before the thought finishes forming."

She opened her mouth, then promptly closed it. The silence stretched, brittle.

Crane leaned in, close enough for her to see the blood vessels in his eyes. "Still think you can handle him?"

Lin wasn't prepared for the briefing to veer toward her sexual vulnerability. A hot flush of defiance reddened her cheeks. "I prefer not to rely on charms," she said, voice even, while emotion warred within her. "I'll get inside his head, if I can, not his bed."

Crane's upper lip twitched, not quite a smile, his eyes assessing her anew. "If you can. Because Kang's mind is a labyrinth, a fortress of diabolical traps. Don't say I didn't warn you."

"Understood."

Crane straightened. "Bok's planning something for the mainland," he said, turning back to the window where storm clouds gathered like artillery smoke. "Small-scale, high-impact—designed to slip through our defenses while the world's watching elsewhere. Kang's running point, which means it's not just an attack. It's a statement. Your job is to get inside, learn the specifics, and stop it if possible."

Crane slid a sleek black folio across the desk, its surface embossed with Russian Doll's discreet insignia. "Your cover," he said, his voice carrying the weight of finality. Inside, Lin found a passport, credit card, driver's license, and a stack of fabricated documents—all bearing the name Dr. Maya Chan. The passport's biometric chip gleamed under the office's harsh light, its pages stamped with a history of travel that never happened. The driver's license listed a Seoul address, its holographic seal flawless. The folio's weight felt heavier than paper and plastic, as if it carried the gravity of a life she'd never lived.

Lin studied the documents, her fingers tracing the passport's embossed cover, committing Maya Chan's details to memory. "Cover identity?" she asked, her voice steady despite the mission's looming stakes.

"Dr. Maya Chan. Biotech consultant, defected after a fabricated Seoul assassination that killed your family. Your mother's background gives you the technical credibility—neural prosthesis expertise, driven by loss and anger against American imperialism. Chan's identity is solid—bank records, publications, a psychology built on resentment."

"How much time do I have to prepare?"

"Not much. You'll have to master it on the flight out."

Crane's gaze hardened. "I won't lie about the odds, Sijue. All three operatives we sent into Black Hand are gone—Dustin Asher, our most valuable asset—missing, presumed dead. We have no idea what happened to him. We just lost another in Taipei, I presume I don't have to tell you about that?"

Lin ignored the barbed question. "What about the third?"

"Harrington." Crane studied her for a reaction. When none came, he said, "I don't think I have to remind you about the dangers of collegial relationships. The price of the dance is never worth the ticket." His eyes flickered to the photograph of his son—a real soldier, lost to a real war. A sacrifice he seemed determined to make obsolete. He turned to the window, the weight of Platform Lazarus itself seeming to settle in his voice. "The Pacific is a powder keg, and every intelligence network from Beijing to Langley knows it. If Bok's planning what I think he is, and we're blind to it, your life serves the mission. That's the equation."

Lin's fingers unconsciously moved to the rhythm of her prayer wheel, its absence a vacuum in her soul. "Understood."

Crane turned back to her, his expression tightened, strategic rather than protective. "Your family's financial security is guaranteed—medical bills, tuition, all of it. But the mission comes first." He gestured toward the door with the casual authority of someone whose smallest movements carried consequence. "Miss Fairweather will take you to processing."

Lin turned and saw Justine Fairweather waiting at the door.

Together they rode the elevator back down into the bowels of the platform.

"It says here, that you are to bring you personal effects to processing," Fairweather said, reading from her tablet.

"Oh?" Lin remarked. "That's unusual."

"I think it's related to your mission. You had better comply."

"No problem."

They stopped by Lin's locker. The only thing of value in it was her grandmother's prayer wheel, which she kept in a traditional silk cross-body bag. It was bundled up with her purse and phone. She grabbed it all and followed Fairweather through a labyrinth of corridors.

Dr. Avery Quinn greeted her with the energy of someone drunk on possibility, his spectacles catching holographic readouts as he moved between displays. "Miss Sijue!" His grin was infectious.

Lin gave him an acidic look. "Just get it over with."

"Of course," Quinn said. He picked up a hypodermic injector gun from a stainless steel tray. "Subdermal tracker. Lift your shirt."

Lin did as she was told.

The injector's pressure capsule ejected its payload with a soft hiss.

Lin flinched but held steady.

Satisfied, Quinn withdrew the injector and wiped away a small bead of blood with an alcohol swab.

"Is that all?" Lin asked.

"Almost," Quinn replied. "Give me your prayer wheel." He reached out his hand, expecting compliance.

Lin gave Quinn a suspicious glare. "It's personal property and none of your business."

Quinn withdrew his hand and reached into his coat pocket. When Lin saw what he produced, she couldn't help but lean forward with curiosity. It was a sleek, lacquered bamboo device, identical in size to her grandmother's prayer wheel but with a modern twist: a 7-centimeter hybrid, its upper half a 4-centimeter prayer wheel engraved with lotus motifs and *Hanja* mantras, its lower half a 3-centimeter pen handle with a subtle *maedeup* knot accent.

Quinn seemed to relish the moment. He clicked a small, knot-styled button atop the wheel, and with a satisfying click, a ballpoint nib extended from the pen's tip. "A functional pen," he said, scribbling a quick mark on his palm to demonstrate. Then, with a deliberate twist of the button 90 degrees and a push, a flush panel on the wheel's side sprang open, revealing a hidden chamber.

Lin leaned closer.

Inside, nestled in a foam-lined slot, were two micro-darts, each 2.5 centimeters long, their metal bodies shaped to mimic the wheel's bearings, their tips sealed in thin film. Lin immediately understood their purpose.

"Sedative darts," he said, anticipating her. "Micro-engineered delivery systems, designed to blend with the wheel's bearings under X-ray. Each one can incapacitate a target in under three seconds—by the time they've yawned, they're asleep." He held out his hand again. "So what do you say?"

This time, Lin slowly retrieved her prayer wheel from her bag. She held it, refusing to surrender it to Quinn, and said, "This is an heirloom handed down from my grandmother. If anything happens to it, you'll regret it."

Quinn's grin widened as he plucked the original from her grip. "Don't worry," he said, "I'll keep it safe until the mission's over. You'll get it back. I promise."

Lin shot him a warning look, almost attempting to snatch it back.

"Go on, spin it," he said. "You'll be surprised."

Lin hefted the counterfeit wheel and spun it. To her surprise, Quinn was right. The ratchet mechanism was smooth, like her original, as if it had been spun thousands of times already.

"We aim to please," Quinn said, pleased with himself.

"I bet you say that to all the girls," Lin replied.

Quinn blushed and looked away, muttering, "Just ... trying to be thorough." Turning back, he smiled sheepishly and pocketed Lin's original prayer wheel. From another pocket, he pulled out something else: a standard hair clip. "Looks ordinary," he said, unlatching the spring and joining the two ends together, "but when you configure it like this, it becomes a blowpipe for the darts."

"Very clever."

"And finally," he said, handing her a wedding ring, "this

contains a nano interceptor programmed to infiltrate their comms network. Loop it over a Cat-9 bundle and it will transmit encrypted data to us. Simple but adaptive, all the while remaining hidden to their IP sniffers."

Lin accepted the ring. It fit perfectly, yet its touch felt alien against her skin.

From another room, Dr. Elana Raskova and Crane watched all this on a monitor. "She's prepared," Raskova told Crane, her gaze fixed on the monitor with a possessiveness that felt both maternal and proprietary.

Later, as the hypersonic transport's engines roared, carrying Lin across the gulf, she pulled out Quinn's counterfeit prayer wheel from her duffle bag and spun it. The replica was perfect, its weight and balance indistinguishable from the heirloom she'd carried for a lifetime. A flawless copy, created in a lab to serve a function. The thought coiled in her gut like a serpent: If they could replace an original that easily ... what was to stop them from doing the same to her? Was she, Lin Sijue, just another asset that could be upgraded, swapped out, and discarded?

– 5 –

The Meeting

Golden Dragon Casino, Macau

THE GOLDEN DRAGON casino breathed decadence. Red silk lanterns swayed in the chilled draft of the ceiling vents, casting flickering shadows over baccarat tables rimmed in lacquered jade. Smoke curled lazily from cigars rolled in Havana but burned in Macau, mingling with the perfume of Shanghai heiresses and Zürich arms dealers. A low wail of *erhu* threaded quietly in the background, imbuing the atmosphere with a sense of longing and loss.

Dr. Maya Chan didn't exist, but she moved like she did.

Lin Sijue's *cheongsam* shimmered in the half-light, emerald silk sliding over muscle honed by her MMA discipline. Her dark hair was pinned high, her Russian Doll comb holding it in place. She glided through crowds of men who measured empires in offshore accounts, women who owned wars without lifting a finger. Every glance Lin returned was weighted, deliberate, inviting curiosity while promising silence. Her hand, almost nervously, went to her lotus leaf cross-body bag, and felt for the Russian Doll prayer wheel, a silent reminder of karma's cycle, grounding her as she wove Maya Chan's facade. In the time she had it, she had spun it regularly and had slowly grown accustomed to its counterfeit facade. It wasn't the same—not by a long shot. But she forced herself to accept it, hoping that in time she might convince herself it was the same.

At Table 8, Kang Hyuk was playing baccarat like a man performing a sacred rite. The charcoal of his bespoke suit clung to a body carved by violence. His face—handsome in a way that resisted softness—remained unreadable as his fingers danced across the cards. His eyes, black-ice sharp, flickered toward Lin as she approached, and for a moment, his fingers paused, a subtle tremor betraying disbelief. She was a mirror to a ghost—Yeon-Hee, his sister, lost to Hamhung's starvation decades ago, her features hauntingly echoed in Lin's high cheekbones and steady gaze.

Lin took the empty seat across from him. A ¥500,000 chip landed at her spot with a practiced flick. She crossed her legs slowly, confidence wrapped in poise, aware of Kang's eyes lingering, searching her face as if chasing a memory. His jaw tightened, a micro-expression of shock he quickly masked, but his gaze returned to her, again and again, like a man caught in a tide.

The table was a gallery of power, its occupants draped in wealth and menace. To Kang's left sat a North African oil heir, mid-twenties, robed in cream linen that whispered of desert fortunes. Sapphire rings weighed his fingers, his expression one of distracted contempt as he flicked chips with a sneer, a young predator testing his claws.

Opposite him was a Eurasian woman in a blood-red pantsuit, her ivory skin stark against the fabric's fire. Her eyes hollow, she stroked a Sphinx cat on her lap, its hairless skin wrinkling as it hissed at anyone who dared to stare at it too long, its yellow gaze mirroring her own—cold, un-yielding.

To Kang's right was an elderly Chinese gentleman, his frail frame at odds with the healthy specimens surrounding him. A watch the size of a grenade was strapped to his gaunt wrist, while an oxygen line clipped to his nose softly hissed with each labored breath. He had been forced to give up smoking years ago and obviously resented it. His fingers moved over his cards with a skittery grace, as if the game needed to be played in a hurry to reclaim the last hours of his life.

Kang's presence was a still-point in the room's ordered chaos. His eyes swept the space in slow, deliberate arcs, missing nothing, but they kept returning to Lin, each glance a struggle to reconcile her with Yeon-Hee's shadow. He met her gaze as she settled, his expression unreadable but not cold—a predator intrigued by a face that stirred buried pain.

The other players noticed her arrival. The oil heir mumbled something unintelligible, his sapphire-ringed eyes flicking over her with a mix of disdain and challenge. The Eurasian woman raised an eyebrow, her cat's tail curling. The old man's lips twitched, briefly revealing a front row of gold teeth, but his focus stayed on his cards. Lin let the tension settle, her ¥500,000 chip a declaration of intent.

"I wonder what tonight brings," she said in flawless Mandarin, her voice light but carrying an edge, like a needle hidden in silk. "I trust you won't mind a touch of competition." A waiter placed a complimentary flute of champagne by her side.

Silence answered, broken only by the dealer's snap of cards, their faces gleaming under the lanterns. The game began, but the real contest was between Lin and Kang, his eyes darting to her with increasing frequency, as if Yeon-Hee's ghost sat across from him.

Lin played with the precision of someone raised on numbers, her bets calculated to draw Kang's interest without overshadowing him. Each card was a step in their silent duet, a flirtation of power and pretense. The other players faded, their stakes and murmurs fading into irrelevance. Kang's fingers hesitated over his chips, his gaze locking on Lin's face, tracing her features—her eyes, her jawline—before snapping back to the game, his control fraying at the edges.

The oil heir folded early, muttering in Arabic as he signaled for a drink. The Eurasian woman's cat closed its eyes as she doubled down, her haughty expression tilted at Lin. The old Chinese man expressed a grimace of disappointment and labored another breath.

Kang matched Lin's tempo, his bets a subtle mirror of hers, though his eyes betrayed his struggle, flickering to her with haunted intensity. "A bold move," he murmured after she doubled her stake on a risky hand, his voice low, a trace of a Korean accent softening his polished Mandarin, tinged with an emotion he couldn't fully mask.

Lin met his gaze, her head cocked slightly. "Sometimes the house isn't the only one allowed to bluff," she replied, her tone a deliberate challenge, testing the crack in his armor.

The table waited. Kang's lips curved, not quite a smile, his eyes lingering on her longer than before, as if seeing Yeon-Hee in every gesture. "Bold words for a newcomer."

"Only if you're afraid of losing," she said, her eyes holding his, flashing a spark of Chan's confidence, though she noted the faint tremor in his hand as he placed his next bet.

The hand played out, and Lin won. The oil heir swore softly, his rings clinking against his glass. The Eurasian woman's face turned sour as she reflexively stroked her cat for comfort. The old Chinese man grumbled unamused, his patience wearing thin.

Kang studied her now, his gaze peeling back layers, heavy with disbelief as Yeon-Hee's resemblance stirred memories he'd buried. "A lack of fear is not always a good thing," he said, his voice quiet, yet curiously controlled, as if wrestling with the ghost before him.

Lin lifted her champagne flute, studying him over the rim. "Depends who is the predator and who is the prey, wouldn't you say?" she said, her tone light but laced with intrigue, aware of his eyes searching her face for answers to a past he couldn't reclaim.

The veins in his neck engorged ever so slightly. "Spoken like a true hunter."

She tilted her head, a tendril of hair brushing her cheek, but didn't say anything. Their eyes momentarily locked, hidden calculations were performed for future reference, then they disengaged. The subtlety of the art was such that even if someone looked, they wouldn't have noticed.

Their next hand began, the rhythm intensifying. Lin's smart-contacts flagged a biometric anomaly—a micro-spike in Kang's pulse, his gaze flickering to her with haunted persistence, as if Yeon-Hee's face haunted his every move. She filed it away, her focus split between his struggle and the table's rhythm.

The room remained tense but calm, chairs creaking as players shifted, murmurs rippling among the crowd. Kang's eyes returned to Lin, his control a thin veneer over the turmoil her resemblance stirred.

To her surprise, however, he won the hand. She realized she had miscalculated. Crane's words came back to her, and she inwardly chastised herself.

While he had his chips gathered up, he said to her, "You play well. A worthy opponent."

Lin smiled and acknowledged his compliment.

Then he said something she *did* expect: "Might I have the pleasure of your company in the rooftop garden? I promise I won't bite."

His voice was silk over steel, a gentleman's invitation with the weight of a command, yet laced with a charm that made refusal feel uncouth. Lin inclined her head, rising with the grace of a panther. "I'd be delighted, is it ...?"

"You can call me Kang."

"Kang it is."

"And you?"

"Maya."

"As in the age-old goddess of illusion?"

"Only to the uninitiated."

He smiled, almost a grin. If she didn't know otherwise,

she would have thought he had showed a sense of boyish youth beneath the veneer, a flicker of vulnerability as Yeon-Hee's shadow lingered in his gaze.

She wordlessly followed him, her senses humming, the casino's chaos fading as they ascended to the rooftop, where the real game awaited.

The rooftop garden was a sanctuary carved from the night, an oasis of quiet elegance above Macau's neon-lit arteries. Marble balustrades gleamed under a crescent moon, framing a *koi* pond where fish glided like liquid amber, their ripples catching the glow of paper lanterns strung across bamboo trellises. The air carried sea salt and ozone, the distant thrum of helicopters mingling with the wind's soft hush, laced with the South China Sea's tang. Below, Macau sprawled like a circuit board, its lights pulsing with restless ambition, a city wired for secrets and betrayal.

Lin stepped into the warm night, her cheongsam catching the breeze, every sense alert. Danger here was subtler than the casino floor—hidden, like invisible radiation. Her smart-contacts scanned for threats, the overlay clear: no immediate hostiles, only faint signatures of surveillance drones high above, scrambled by the casino's countermeasures. Russian Doll's training whispered: The quietest moments hide the sharpest knives

Kang stood by a lacquered bar near the pond, his silhouette a study in control, though his eyes flicked to her

with a haunted intensity, as if Yeon-Hee's ghost stood before him. He dismissed the bartender with a nod, turning
with two glasses of amber liquid catching the lanternlight.
As he approached, Lin's sharp eyes caught a subtle irregularity in his gait—a faint waddle, nearly imperceptible, as if
his left leg lagged ever so slightly. The raised undersole of
his left shoe, discreetly thicker to compensate for a shorter
leg, betrayed the effort he'd mastered to conceal it. Kang
shifted his weight onto his good leg, steadying himself with
practiced ease, his posture flawless by the time he reached
her. "Ms. Chan," he said, his voice smooth as aged whiskey,
though a faint tremor betrayed his struggle to reconcile her
face with Yeon-Hee's memory. "Something strong to match
your nerve."

Lin accepted the glass, her fingers brushing his with
calculated precision, her observation of his gait filed away
without a flicker of acknowledgment. The liquor's peaty
bite hit her nose—Laphroaig 25, harsh and unforgiving,
a test of pain's embrace. She sipped, the burn searing her
throat, but her expression remained serene, a graceful defiance. Kang's eyes flickered with approval, a predator noting
resilience, yet clouded by the ghost of his sister.

"To high stakes," he said, raising his glass, his gaze locked
on hers, searching her features as if to confirm or deny the
impossible.

Lin clinked hers, the crystal chiming softly. "Only if

they're calculated." She held his stare, Maya Chan's confidence a shield for Lin's calculations.

They settled at a low table by the koi pond, Macau's neon haze below, the lanterns casting a warm glow across their faces. Kang leaned back, his posture relaxed but his eyes sharp, a predator at ease but never off guard, his gaze flickering to Lin's face with a haunted persistence. Taking her cue, he said, "You mustn't think gambling is my life's work, Ms. Chan. It's a side hustle, mere entertainment. I never wager the principal—only the profits. A man must have control, wouldn't you agree?"

Lin tilted her head, her ivory comb catching the light. "Discipline stands out in a place like this. So what's your real work, Mr. Kang?" Her tone was light, but her smart-contacts flagged a micro-spike in his body temperature—anticipation, tinged with the turmoil of Yeon-Hee's resemblance.

He smiled, a closed door with a crack of invitation. "Something less … visible. But first, tell me about yourself. Your family, perhaps? What shaped a woman who moves like a shadow and strikes like a viper?"

Lin felt the probe, her breathing steady as she crafted the lie. She let her gaze drift to the koi pond, a flicker of vulnerability in her eyes—a performance honed by Russian Doll. "I grew up in Beijing, near the Summer Palace. My father was a biophysicist, brilliant but distant, lost in equations. My mother … she had ALS, diagnosed when I was twelve. Watching her body betray her—her voice fading, her hands stilling—it carved something in me. I turned to neural prostheses, wanting to give people like her a chance to move, to speak, to live again. But the government saw tools, not lives. They buried her case to protect their image, betrayed us for their own ends."

Kang's eyes softened, a predator scenting a shared wound, his gaze lingering on her face as if Yeon-Hee's features stirred a deeper ache. "Betrayal cuts deeper than any blade," he said, his voice low, his fingers tightening briefly on his glass. "You left China because of it?"

Lin nodded, her lie seamless but heavy, the prayer wheel her anchor. "I went to the West, chasing a dream of science without shackles, but found the same lies—bureaucrats who cared more for control than cures. So here I am, looking for a place to build something real." She sipped her Laphroaig, its harshness grounding her, and turned the probe back. "And you, Mr. Kang? What drives a man who gambles only for sport?"

His gaze drifted to the city's neon veins, a crack in his armor widening, Yeon-Hee's shadow deepening his pause. "My family …" He paused, the words heavy, as if dredged from a buried place. "I come from the North, Ms. Chan— Hamhung, a city of smoke and steel. My parents, my sister, they perished in factories, starved and worked to death. I was ten, scrounging for scraps while they faded. The world called it economics; I call it murder, orchestrated by American sanctions that choked us to our knees. That kind of loss … it teaches you the cost of weakness."

Lin raised her eyebrows, her expression a careful blend of surprise and empathy, knowing her resemblance to Yeon-Hee amplified his vulnerability. "North Korea? Yet you're here, a man of means, far from home. How does one rise like that?"

Kang's smile returned, sharp but warm, a man dancing on the edge of revelation, his eyes flickering to her face as if seeking confirmation of the impossible. "I work for my government, high up. They trust me to move where others cannot, to secure what we need—strength, independence, a future unchained. Freedom, Ms. Chan, isn't given. It's taken."

She leaned closer, her voice soft but probing. "So you're not military, but …" She let the question hang, a velvet trap.

He chuckled, deflecting with practiced ease, the koi rippling below as if sensing the shift. "Let's say my work involves … delicate operations. High stakes, high rewards—a certain excitement for those with the nerve." His eyes gleamed, peeling back her facade, haunted by her likeness to his sister. "We're always looking for talent—people who see through the world's lies, who don't flinch at shadows."

Lin's smart-contacts caught a spike in his muscle tension—excitement, ambition, and the turmoil of Yeon-Hee's ghost. She tilted her head, a tendril of hair brushing her cheek. "Is this a job interview, Mr. Kang?"

His laugh echoed over the pond, rich and unguarded, a flicker of boyish warmth breaking through as he grappled with her resemblance. "Only if you want it to be, Ms. Chan. I see potential in you—rare, like a flame that burns without flickering. But potential needs a purpose."

She sipped her Laphroaig, its burn a steady anchor, letting the pause stretch. "And what purpose would that be? I don't even know who you work for."

Kang leaned back, his fingers tracing the rim of his glass, the city's neon reflecting in his eyes, his gaze flickering to her face with haunted insistence. "A group that thrives in discretion. We deal in possibilities—networks, technologies, futures others fear to touch. Your neural prostheses, for instance—imagine them unbound by red tape, reshaping lives, rewriting rules. We're building a world where strength, not submission, defines progress."

Lin's mind raced, filing away the hint of Black Hand, the covert North Korean agency rumored to weave espionage and tech into a shadow empire. She pressed gently, her tone curious but measured. "A bold vision. Could I meet your employer, see this world for myself?"

Kang's smile was wily, a fox slipping a snare, though his eyes betrayed a flicker of longing as he studied her features. "My employers prefer the shadows, Ms. Chan. Direct meetings are... impractical. But I could show you where I work—a glimpse of what's possible. Would that interest you?"

Her mission hummed: infiltrate, uncover, survive. She nodded, her expression intrigued but controlled. "It would. When?"

Kang leaned forward, his voice a velvet invitation, tinged with the weight of Yeon-Hee's memory. "Tomorrow, perhaps. But first, let's continue this over a late-night tea—there's an exclusive tea house in Coloane, intimate, perfect for deeper conversations."

Lin tilted her head, deflecting with a smile. "Tempting, but jet lag's catching up. I need sleep to keep my edge. Tomorrow, then?"

He nodded, approval flickering in his eyes, softened by the ghost of his sister. "Tomorrow." He reached into his suit, producing a matte black business card with silver lettering.

Lin accepted it with a subtle bow of her head. The writing was in Hangul and English: *Chosun Precision Components, Kang Hyuk, Director of Acquisitions.* Below, a tagline: *Empowering the Future through Innovation.*

"My work," Kang said, his tone casual but weighted, "involves sourcing specialized components for the DPRK's Bureau of Scientific Advancement—parts to modernize our industries, to stand independent against those who'd starve us again."

Lin slipped the card into her cross-body. "Independence is a powerful motivator, Mr. Kang. I look forward to seeing your world."

"I'd very much appreciate that," Kang responded. "Say, tomorrow, downstairs by the entrance foyer?"

"I can do that. But if something comes up ..."

"I can still find you," Kang said. "There's a tracker in the card."

"Of course."

Kang raised his glass, his toast a seal, his eyes lingering on her face as if Yeon-Hee's shadow held him captive. "To new beginnings, Ms. Chan."

She clinked her glass against his, the crystal chiming softly. "To possibilities."

They stood, Kang moving toward the balustrade with a measured stride, the faint waddle reappearing briefly as he adjusted his weight, only to vanish as he leaned against the marble. The wind stirred the lanterns, the koi rippling below. Kang extended his hand, a gentleman's gesture with a killer's weight. Lin took it, her grip firm, his warmth hiding strength that could crush or create. The city flickered below, a circuit poised to burn, and the stars above watched, silent as the ghosts of their pasts. The wheel of karma turned, and Lin stepped closer to the fire.

Her hand unconsciously brushed the prayer wheel in

her bag, Lin Sijue's anchor in Maya Chan's performance. A counterfeit like her, but like Maya, the distinction between real and fake was slowly blurring.

She smiled, or rather, Maya smiled, allowing anticipation to touch her features. "I'd be very interested to see that, Mr. Kang."

– 6 –

The Compound

Black Hand Facility
Liaoning Province, China

T HE GOLDEN DRAGON's entrance foyer shimmered beneath a canopy of crystal chandeliers, their prisms fracturing light into fleeting rainbows across polished marble floors. Lin Sijue stood at the appointed hour, her emerald *cheongsam* from the previous night replaced by a sleek black ensemble—tailored jacket, fitted trousers, boots with silent soles—crafted for whatever lay beyond Macau's neon veil. The air carried the salty taste of the South China Sea and mingled with the understated hint of perfume she decided to apply before leaving her hotel room, a Jo Malone, Wood & Sage, version three.

Her smart-contacts swept the foyer, flagging a black van idling at the curb, its tinted windows opaque, engine humming with restrained menace. But before she could catalog the van's license plate, rough hands seized her from behind, their grip professional but unyielding. "Dr. Chan?" The voice was flat, stripped of warmth, a soldier's cadence in clipped Mandarin.

Lin's Russian Doll training held her response in check, her body relaxed to avoid signaling resistance. "That's me," she said, her tone measured, Maya Chan's curiosity laced with just enough unease to sell the persona.

A canvas hood descended, plunging her into darkness, the coarse fabric grazing her cheeks. Her left hand brushed against the familiar weight of her brass prayer wheel, tucked in cross-body pressed against her hip as she was hustled into the van. The engine roared to life, its rumble blending with muffled Mandarin exchanges among her captors—three, perhaps four, their voices low but taut, as if braced for trouble.

Four hours passed in the hood's stifling embrace. Lin counted the turns, her training cataloging each shift: forty-seven minutes on smooth highway asphalt, then a jarring lurch onto gravel, followed by winding mountain routes where the van swayed against steep inclines. The air grew cooler, thinner, the sea's tang fading into pine and dust. Her smart-contacts, dimmed to conserve power, recorded micro-vibrations, estimating a northeast trajecto-ry—Liaoning Province, likely, a region riddled with aban-doned mines and clandestine facilities.

The van lurched to a stop, and the hood was ripped away, leaving Lin blinking against the harsh glare of sodi-um floodlights. Her senses reeled, assaulted by a cocktail of chemical fumes—sulfur compounds, industrial solvents, the acrid bite of battery acid mingling with something or-ganic, putrid, like rotting kelp. The cold mountain air bit at her skin, her exhales misting in the chill, while genera-tors hummed in the distance, their mechanical heartbeat throbbing through the rocky ground like a diseased circu-latory system. The vibrations traveled up through her boot soles, a constant reminder of the compound's subterranean vastness.

Carved into Liaoning's cliffs, the compound wore the mask of a derelict mine—rusted cranes and ore carts staged with theatrical precision, too pristine for disuse, a decoy for satellite eyes. But beneath the facade, the facility breathed with purpose: organized, fortified, alive. The air was heavy with the scent of electrical insulation pushed to dangerous limits. A waft of cordite carried on the wind, which seemed at this very moment to whip itself up, as if it wanted to whisper something urgent.

The sky above was bruised purple, storm clouds swelling like an angry wound. Lightning flickered on the horizon, its flash echoing the unease coiling in Lin's chest. She tasted ozone on her tongue, and felt the hairs stand up on her forearm, while the approaching thunder made the mountain itself seem to groan in anticipation.

"Welcome to the real world, Dr. Chan." Kang Hyuk's voice was silk over steel as he emerged from the shadows, his bespoke charcoal suit immaculate despite the industrial grit. His eyes held the calculating patience of a chess master, each glance cataloging her reactions with surgical precision. They seemed to say: No empires here. No lies.

Lin summoned Maya Chan's persona, letting her eyes widen with manufactured wonder while her trained gaze swept the compound's vulnerabilities: rusted ventilation grates half-concealed by scrub, exposed wiring where hasty construction had cut corners, security cameras with blind spots that spoke of either laziness or deliberate oversight. Her smart-contacts flagged a drone's faint heat signature high above, its signal scrambled by countermeasures.

"Impressive," she said, her voice carrying a breathless note of admiration, carefully calculated to stroke Kang's ego. "I had no idea your operation was so … comprehensive." Kang's smile was predatory, a flash of teeth that promised no mercy. She caught a flicker in his expression—the way his pupils dilated slightly at the sound municipalities, her voice, a micro-expression of a man filing away every data point, every gesture, building a psychological profile in real time. He was studying her as intently as she was studying him. "Follow me."

As Kang led the way, his measured stride betrayed the faint waddle only in fleeting moments—when he navigated a slight incline in the concrete corridor, the raised sole of his shoe triggering a slight hitch in his rhythm. Lin noted it without shifting her gaze. Their footsteps echoed through concrete corridors lit by flickering fluorescents, the electrical buzz a constant drone that burrowed into Lin's skull.

Left turn past the ventilation grate—rusted hinges, loose screws. Emergency exit potential, she catalogued automatically, her Russian Doll training fully engaged. *Right at the intersection—security camera blind spot where the pipes create shadow coverage.*

The walls were stark, utilitarian, but she noted subtle tells of recent expansion—paint too fresh in patches, concrete too clean where new tunnels had been carved from the mountain's bones. The air grew heavier, laced with the metallic tang of recycled oxygen and the sweet-sour smell of industrial lubricants, a reminder of the compound's subterranean depths. Her breath formed small clouds in the chill, and she felt the mountain's weight pressing down, kilometers of stone between her and freedom.

They passed multiple security checkpoints, each manned by guards in black tactical gear, their eyes tracking Lin with professional wariness. Her cover as Dr. Maya Chan, biotech consultant, held under their scrutiny, but the weight of their gazes pressed against her like a physical force. She kept her posture relaxed, her expression one of curious deference, while her mind cataloged their weapons—Type 95 rifles, biometric scanners, neural stunners clipped to belts. The guards' positioning spoke of military training, but she noticed subtle tells: one favored his left shoulder, another's stance suggested an old knee injury. Even elite soldiers carried vulnerabilities.

Kang indicated a full body scanner, its red light sweeping an arc like a predator's gaze. "Standard security protocol," he said, his tone too casual for the compound's paranoia. "I'm sure you understand."

Lin stepped in, its crimson beam playing across her body like searching fingers. She braced herself, recalling the card scanner's analysis of Kang's chip, which had flagged an embedded signal protocol—likely a tracker or authentication key. If her prayer wheel's quantum chip, upgraded on Platform Lazarus, carried a similar signal, it might trigger the scanner. She trusted the darts—camouflaged as bearings—would evade even an X-ray's gaze. The machine's tone shifted, a subtle beep confirming her suspicion about the chip.

Inviting her out on the other side, Kang said, "Something in your bag, Dr. Chan?" His voice carried steel beneath the silk, a challenge veiled in courtesy.

Lin's hand moved smoothly to her cross-body bag. She

reached into a silk-lined pouch, producing the prayer wheel with practiced casualness—a 7-centimeter device, its upper half a 4-centimeter lacquered bamboo prayer wheel engraved with Hanja mantras and lotus patterns, its lower half a 3-centimeter pen handle with a maedeup knot accent. "A gift from my grandmother," she said, letting sentimentality color her voice—a touch of embarrassment, a hint of vulnerability, Maya Chan's humanity on display. She gripped the pen handle in her palm, flicking the wheel with her thumb to spin it briefly, the mantras blurring like a prayer in motion.

Kang took the prayer wheel, his fingers tracing its engraved lotus patterns with deliberate care. He noticed the button atop the wheel, styled like a polished maedeup knot, and pressed it. A satisfying "click" sounded as the pen nib extended from the handle's tip. He scribbled a quick mark on his palm, a faint smirk crossing his lips at the functional pen. He spun the wheel with his thumb, its ratchet sound echoing faintly, then produced a handheld scanner with his other hand. Its light probed the bamboo surface, and a faint beep echoed—anomaly detected, likely the quantum chip. Kang's thumb hovered over the button a second longer—then released. He ran the scanner again, slower. No beep. He shrugged, chalking it up to a quirk of the device, a false positive.

"Superstitious?" he asked, his eyes narrowing, a flicker of

suspicion beneath his charm.

Lin's voice was soft, steady. "My grandmother's faith, nothing more." She held her gaze, her breathing even, the lie seamless despite the weight of his scrutiny. The dart chamber, its sedative darts disguised as bearings behind a flush panel, remained locked—Kang hadn't twisted the button to access it.

After a long moment, Kang handed the prayer wheel back, his expression unreadable but tinged with what might have been approval—or calculation. "Family is important," he said. "It reminds us what we're fighting for."

Lin nodded, tucking the prayer wheel back into her cross-body's pouch with reverent care, her mind noting the scanner's sensitivity. The quantum chip had nearly betrayed her; she'd need to recalibrate its emissions before the next checkpoint. But the darts, hidden in plain sight, had passed unnoticed, an insurance policy against what she dared not imagine.

Kang led her through a wide corridor to some doors, swiped his card. The doors opened to reveal a cavernous space, a sterile labyrinth of glass and steel where scientists in hazmat suits moved with tense precision. Glowing vials lined workstations, their contents shimmering with unnatural hues—bio-accelerants, Lin assumed, recalling Kang's promises of possibilities unbound by bureaucracy and whispers of biological replication she'd overheard on

Platform Lazarus. The chemical stench assaulted her nostrils, a caustic blend of laboratory disinfectant and a darker, organic edge, like blood and decay. Neural interface rigs loomed at the wing's edges, their cables snaking into servers that hummed with quiet menace, their design chillingly familiar: almost certainly the un-hackable neurotechnology stolen by Finger in Taipei, now repurposed for Black Hand's ambitions.

The command center was a cavern carved from living rock, its walls ablaze with holographic displays that shimmered with malevolent intent. Red vectors traced Black Hand's global reach: operatives embedded in Jakarta's financial district, weapons caches buried in Tokyo's underground, a submarine lurking off Vancouver's coast. The scope was breathtaking, a spider's web of influence that dwarfed the casino's decadence and rivaled Russian Doll's surveillance. But one display made Lin's blood freeze—real-time CCTV feeds from U.S. infrastructure: oil refineries in Texas, their pipelines glowing under infrared; power plants in California, their turbines humming; water purification facilities in New York, their control rooms monitored via hacked feeds. Data links flickered with intercepted traffic—maintenance logs, security rotations, system vulnerabilities—revealing a network poised to cripple a nation's lifelines, despite quantum-encrypted protections shielding their core systems.

Kang stood at the center, his presence commanding, his head held high with pride. "Governments hide behind quantum encryption now, believing their systems untouchable," he said, his voice carrying the cold authority of absolute conviction. "But no code is stronger than human weakness. Loose lips sink ships, Dr. Chan. We don't waste time cracking quantum networks; we turn insiders—technicians, guards, executives—people who carry the data in their heads. The source is always the softest target."

Lin's response was instinctive, a perfect blend of curiosity and unease honed by Russian Doll's training. "You mean sabotage through … people?"

Kang nodded, his eyes never leaving her face, quickening with a micro-expression of satisfaction—her reaction was exactly what he expected. "Control is about leverage, not just technology. A bribed engineer or a coerced operator gives us more than any intercepted transmission ever could."

Lin, as Maya Chan, maintained a high level of attentiveness, showing she was absorbing what he was saying.

Kang approved and continued his tour.

In the bio-research wing, a sealed chamber had caught her eye, its glass frosted but not enough to hide a humanoid silhouette within, its features blurred by cold vapor. The figure was perfectly still, suspended in amniotic fluid, tubes and cables connected to its motionless form. Kang's voice was casual, almost mocking. "Let our rivals waste their time building perfect servants. We build survivors. And survivors do what is necessary to win." The words landed like a stone in still water, rippling through Lin's thoughts, stirring Peter's revelation of cloning, first voiced in Shanghai's neon rain.

"Why are you showing me this?" she asked, her voice carefully measured, Maya Chan's persona intact. "Surely you know that cloning has been internationally banned by the United Nations?"

Kang gave her a curious look. Then it passed and he smiled. "You're right. We should just cower in the corner and let the super powers fuck us up the ass."

"I didn't mean it like that."

"How did you mean it?"

Lin felt Kang's stare bearing down on her, hot as a blowtorch. She tried to remember what Brad had told her. Don't defend. Attack. "I agree. You have every right to play them at their own game. But is that the game they're playing?"

Kang had to think twice before answering. It was clearly not what he expected.

Lin could see that he was calculating what to say. How much should he give away?

Carefully, and with the reserve of a man who had nearly been bitten by a venomous snake, Kang said, "As I explained, our clones are not slaves. First and foremost, they're for medical research. But don't fool yourself. If we didn't do it, someone else would—they are—and so we are not doing anything except keeping up with the Jones."

"If your clones are free, then why do you need someone like me, with expertise in neural implants?"

Kang nodded impatiently. "Free is a relative term Dr. Chan. We can't risk our clones in public without keeping them on a leash. Surely you can appreciate that?"

"Yes ..."

Kang flashed her a business-like smile. "Come, we're not finished yet."

He led her to a large mess hall, where hundreds of workers were filtering in and out to eat from a large bouffet-style service counter.

Kang ushered her to the queue.

The mess hall was a cavernous expanse, its steel tables scarred from years of use, lined with workers in drab gray uniforms, their movements mechanical, faces etched with the quiet endurance of survival. Harsh fluorescent strips buzzed overhead, their light cold and flickering, casting stark shadows across the concrete floor. The air was heavy with the steam of boiled grains and the sharp tang of fermentation, undercut by the faint metallic bite of recycled oxygen, a reminder of the compound's subterranean isolation. The distant hum of generators pulsed through the walls, syncing with the muffled crash of waves against Liaoning's cliffs, a rhythm as relentless as the mission Lin carried.

Kang handed her a dented metal tray, gesturing toward the buffet counter where stainless steel bins steamed under the fluorescents. The spread was sparse, designed for sustenance, not indulgence—food for North Korean workers, rooted in the austerity of a nation that had long prioritized function over flavor. Bowls of *kongbap*, a gritty mix of rice and beans, sat beside heaps of *kimchi*, its fiery red cabbage glistening with chili paste. Strips of *danmuji*, pickled radish, offered a pale yellow contrast, while *miyeokguk*, a thin seaweed soup, shimmered in shallow vats, its broth cloudy but fragrant. A tray of *japchae*, stir-fried glass noodles tangled with wilted vegetables, rested next to watery *mandu* dumplings, their dough sagging under the weight of meager fillings. A small platter of *bulgogi*, thinly sliced beef marinated in soy, was reserved for senior staff, its aroma a rare hint of richness in the utilitarian spread.

Lin hesitated, her tray cold in her hands, her Seoul upbringing clashing with Maya Chan's fabricated Beijing roots. She scanned the options, calculating her choice to reinforce her cover. *Bulgogi* was too elite, a signal of privilege that didn't fit Dr. Chan's narrative of betrayal and defection. *Kongbap* and *kimchi* were safe, humble staples that aligned with her story of loss and resilience. She spooned a modest portion of the grainy rice onto her tray, adding a small mound of *kimchi* for its sharp familiarity and a bowl of *miyeokguk* for its warmth, and in the last minutes quickly adding some *japchae*, which she couldn't help, being one of her favorites, her movements deliberate to blend with the workers' quiet efficiency. Her fingers brushed the prayer wheel in her cross-body bag, its lacquered bamboo a counterfeit anchor, its weight grounding her as she wove Maya Chan's persona tighter. The wheel wasn't her grandmother's, but its smooth spin had become a ritual, a tether to Lin Sijue beneath the lie.

As she turned from the counter, a woman approached, her lab coat crisp against the mess hall's drabness, her sharp features framed by a tight bun of black hair. Her eyes, cold and analytical, locked onto Lin with the precision of a targeting laser. Kang's posture shifted, a flicker of pride softening his predatory edge. "Dr. Chan, meet my sister, Dr. Soo-Min Kang, our lead neurovirologist," he said, his voice carrying a note of official respect tinged with a hint of personal warmth. "She's the mind behind our neural integration projects."

Lin's heart stuttered, her mind racing as she processed the introduction. Another sister? Crane's briefing on Kang had detailed Yeon-Hee's death—starvation in Hamhung, a wound that shaped Kang's hatred—but no mention of another sibling. Was this an oversight, a deliberate omission, or something darker? Her Russian Doll training kicked in, cataloging possibilities: Soo-Min could be a recent addition to Black Hand, her role concealed from Russian Doll's intelligence; or perhaps Crane withheld the information to test Lin's adaptability, a need-to-know tactic typical of his games. Worse, Soo-Min's existence might hint at deeper secrets—cloning, manipulation, a family reconstructed in Black Hand's labs. The thought chilled her, Peter's warnings about cloning echoing from their clandestine meeting in Platform Lazarus's blind spot. She buried the unease, summoning Maya Chan's confidence, her expression one of polite curiosity. "Likewise, Dr. Kang. Your work sounds … ambitious," she said, her tone light but measured, her smart-contacts flagging a micro-spike in Soo-Min's pulse—anticipation, suspicion, or both.

-Min's handshake was firm, devoid of warmth, like gripping a steel tool. "A pleasure, Dr. Chan," she said, her Mandarin clipped, her eyes searching for cracks in Lin's facade. "Hyuk tells me you're an expert in neural prostheses. I look forward to learning from you." The words were polite, but the undertone was a challenge, a scalpel poised to cut.

They moved to a table, trays clinking against the steel surface, the mess hall's din a shield for their conversation. Over lunch, Soo-Min wasted no time, her questions slicing through the meal like a blade. "Dr. Chan, how do you address glial scarring in long-term neural implants?" she asked, her voice clinical, her chopsticks poised over her kongbap as if the food were an afterthought.

Lin chewed a bite of *kimchi*, its heat grounding her, and answered with the precision of her mother's biotech lectures. "Polyethylene glycol coatings on electrodes reduce inflammation, minimizing scar tissue while promoting neural integration." She sipped her *miyeokguk*, its salty warmth steadying her nerves, her response textbook but convincing.

Soo-Min's eyes narrowed, unsatisfied but pressing further. "And neurotransmitter imbalances post-implantation? How do you stabilize synaptic firing?" Her tone was sharper now, a probe seeking weaknesses.

Lin leaned back, her posture relaxed but her mind racing. "GABA receptor agonists to dampen overexcitation, paired with low-frequency stimulation to mimic natural neural patterns." Her answer drew on Russian Doll's crash course, solid enough to hold under scrutiny. The *japchae* on her tray sat untouched, its noodles congealing as she focused on Soo-Min's relentless interrogation.

The questions escalated, each one more technical, a gauntlet designed to expose fraud. "What about astrocyte signaling? How do you prevent feedback loops from destabilizing implants?" Soo-Min's chopsticks tapped her tray, a metronome of impatience.

Lin countered smoothly, her training holding firm. "Calcium wave suppression via targeted inhibitors, like minocycline, to stabilize astrocyte-neuron interactions." She met Soo-Min's gaze, her expression one of professional curiosity, though her pulse quickened under the neurovirologist's scrutiny.

Soo-Min's final question was a surgical strike, her voice deceptively calm. "And T-cell mediated rejection of neural probes—specifically, how do you address CD8+ cytotoxic activity?" Her eyes gleamed, a predator sensing blood.

Lin hesitated, her mind scrambling for an answer. Her preparation hadn't covered this niche corner of immunology, a field so specialized it demanded years of study, not the hours she'd had since leaving Platform Lazarus. "Immunosuppressive coatings," she said, her voice steady but vague, "to minimize T-cell activation and protect the probe's interface." It was a weak deflection, a general truth that skirted the specifics.

Soo-Min's lips thinned, her correction swift and sharp. "CD8+ T-cells require targeted HLA modulation to prevent cytotoxic attacks on probes. That's foundational immunology for neural implant specialists, Dr. Chan." Her tone was ice, her eyes locked on Lin, cataloging the misstep.

Kang, finishing his *mandu*, chuckled, dismissing the tension. "Always the perfectionist, Soo-Min. Let Dr. Chan eat in peace." He assumed his sister's sharpness was jealousy, a sibling rivalry fueled by Lin's resemblance to Yeon-Hee, but his eyes flickered with a trace of unease, a crack in his confidence.

Lin forced a smile, her heart pounding as she sipped her soup, the seaweed's tang masking her unease. She'd weathered the storm, but Soo-Min's correction exposed a gap she couldn't afford. The prayer wheel pressed against her hip, its spin a silent mantra: Karma returns, always.

As they finished, the trio rose, slotting their trays into the cleaning shelves, the metal racks clanging with each addition. A worker nearby fumbled his tray, the crash of *kimchi* splattering across the floor drawing Lin's gaze. The man, gaunt and nervous, scrambled to clean it, muttering apologies in Korean as guards loomed. Right or wrong, Lin crouched down and helped him. She gathered up his chopsticks which had skittered across the floor and returned them too him. She looked for a spoon which she saw slide under a nearby table. There were some people there who joined in the search.

In that moment, Soo-Min pulled Kang aside, her voice low, urgent, hidden by the stack of trays. "Maya Chan's an impostor. The CD8+ T-cell response should be basic knowledge for someone familiar with immunology. I don't trust her. She's not who she says she is."

Kang's jaw tightened, his gaze flicking to Lin as she watched the worker's cleanup, her profile a haunting echo of Yeon-Hee's. "Maybe she was nervous, or maybe you're seeing ghosts because she looks like her," he snapped, his voice a low growl. "Yeon-Hee's gone, Soo-Min. Don't let your paranoia sabotage this. She's an asset."

Soo-Min's eyes flashed, her restraint fraying. She nearly accused him of letting Yeon-Hee's ghost cloud his judgment but bit back the words. Instead, she pressed, her tone cold as the compound's air. "Test her yourself, Hyuk. Don't let sentiment blind you. If she's real, she'll pass. If not, we can't risk it—not with the project this close."

Kang's fingers twitched, clenching briefly into a fist before relaxing, his gaze lingering on Lin's profile, her resemblance to Yeon-Hee a quiet ache. "Fine," he said, his voice steel wrapped in silk. "I have just the test to prove you right or wrong. Tomorrow, in the lab. If she's a fraud, I'll know."

Soo-Min nodded, her expression unyielding, and stepped back as Lin rejoined them, her tray slotted, her posture relaxed but her eyes alert. Kang forced a smile, his charm seamless. "Ready to continue, Dr. Chan? The lab awaits." His tone was warm, but Lin caught the flicker in his eyes—a calculation, a shift from the rooftop's haunted intensity. Her smart-contacts flagged a micro-spike in his pulse, a tell she filed away.

They moved toward the exit, the mess hall's din fading behind them, replaced by the thrum of generators and whoosh of fans pushing air. Lin's hand brushed the prayer wheel, its counterfeit spin a reminder of her own duality—

Lin Sijue beneath Maya Chan, truth beneath lies. Soo-Min's suspicion was a blade at her throat, and Kang's looming test a shadow she couldn't outrun. The compound's corridors stretched ahead, a labyrinth of steel and secrets, each step drawing her deeper into Black Hand's web. The wheel of karma turned, its rhythm relentless, and Lin braced for the fire to come.

– 7 –

Loyalty Test

Black Hand Facility
Liaoning Province, China

THE fluorescent lights in the detention sub-level buzzed like dying insects, casting harsh, stuttering shadows across bare concrete walls. A chemical reek clung to everything—part bleach, part something burnt and organic that lodged in the back of Lin's throat and refused to leave. She followed Kang in silence, trying not to think too hard, just memorize the twists and turns he took through the tunnel passages that made her feel like they had become rats in a maze.

"You've proven yourself capable, Dr. Chan," Kang said, his voice metallic against the hallway's reverb. "But capability and loyalty are different currencies in my organization."

Lin kept her expression calm, measured. She knew the North Korean patriarchal system well. Trust was earned, not given. No doubt, some sort of loyalty test was coming. This usually meant drinking alarming quantities of *soju* or *baekseju*—strong herbal infusions often touted for their medicinal properties—while regaling the group with tales of outsmarting the enemy. The stories were dissected and challenged, their details prodded ad infinitum until the interlocutor was satisfied of their authenticity.

Kang stopped before a steel door stamped with faded Korean characters. He rubbed his hands together absentmindedly, his voice dropping. "Personal experience has taught me that betrayal always comes from those closest to you. Whether in love or war ... I'm sure you'd agree."

The door groaned open to the sound of scraping metal.

Inside: a windowless chamber, all concrete and unnaturally silent. A single steel chair occupied the center. Shackled to it, slumped forward, was a man.

Lin froze.

It was Peter.

A single factory lamp above him flooded him in a cone of harsh light while the rest of the room faded into murky shadows.

Their meeting in Shanghai came flooding back. It was as if he had just stepped out of their capsule hotel and returned. His chin was slumped to his chest, his hair matted with oily sweat, his cheeks shadowed by several days' growth—but otherwise, this was the Peter she knew in every detail. Right down to the small mole on the right side of his neck, now exposed and torn raw from some unspeakable torture.

"A gift from our benefactors," Kang said, pacing like a surgeon about to make the first incision. "Russian Doll has been generous. This one claimed he was hunting Black Hand operatives in Taipei. Said he was looking for Lin Sijue."

The shock of seeing Peter before her very eyes almost drowned out Kang's indirect admission that this was a Black Hand operation. Two pieces of information dumped on her in the same instant. No doubt Kang had planned this for maximum impact, and Lin fought against every muscle and nerve fiber in her body not to react, to remain impassive, not give him anything to raise suspicion. *Lin Sijue, how clever!* But she was not Lin Sijue; she was Dr Maya Chan! And this is what she gave him, momentarily catching Kang's shifty gaze without flinching before setting her eyes on Peter, expressionless, drained of emotion, as if she had bleached all the color from the world.

Peter raised his head, slowly. A thin surgical scar peeked out from behind the left ear. To the trained eye, it would almost be unnoticeable. But not to hers. She knew Peter ...

he doesn't have a scar there. I've kissed that spot a hundred times. Traced every inch of his neck with my fingers.

Her mind reeled. She remembered what Peter had told her, had warned her about. Yet ... here he was. The love of her life!

With almost superhuman effort, she got a hold of herself. She pushed away the emotional turmoil and focused on the analytical voice in the back of her brain. *Neural implant site*, she concluded. *Just like Sebastian Clay's scar in Taipei. They didn't just capture Peter—they copied him.*

But how perfect! His strong but gentle hands. The hair on his forearms. The color of his skin.

Kang callously grabbed a bunch of hair on the top of Peter's head and yanked his head up so that his face was directly angled at Lin.

One of his eyes was half shut from swelling, a dark purple bruise had gathered beneath it like a storm cloud. Blood trickled from his nose. His lower lip was split and more blood oozed from the open wound.

But even through the damage, even through the pain and fear written across his features, Lin could see the subtle differences now that she knew to look. The way his good eye tracked movement was slightly off—too calculating, like software processing rather than human intuition. The micro-expressions were perfect, but they felt rehearsed, programmed.

He believes he's Peter, she understood with sickening clarity. *They've implanted him with Peter's memories, his emotions, his love for me. That's what makes this so monstrous—he genuinely thinks he's dying for love.*

Kang motioned to a goon who had been standing back in the shadows. A bucket of ice cold water was unceremoniously flung at Peter's face.

Peter jerked back against his restraints, his good eye blinked open.

For a moment Lin's own eyes engaged with his.

Was that a flash of recognition? A brief moment of secret connection then stone cold withdrawal, professional training to prevent compromise?

"Do you know this man?" Kang asked, intuiting something but not quite putting his finger on it.

"No," Lin shook her head adamantly. "I've never seen him before in my life."

The lie tasted like copper and ash.

"In that case ..." Kang withdrew his sidearm and placed it in her hand. The metal was warm—sickeningly human. "Prove your loyalty. Kill him."

The room tilted for a moment.

Lin had killed only once before. A necessary action. Self-defense in the heat of combat. But this. A deliberate, premeditated execution at close range ...

"Something wrong?" Kang asked, almost fatherly.

"No," Lin said. "I was just thinking, is there something you haven't learned from him yet? Would it be a waste to kill him when perhaps I could extract something from him?"

"Be my guest," Kang said, folding his arms, as if unconvinced but willing to see it out.

Lin leaned in close and pushed the barrel of the gun against Peter's temple. It was a ploy, she knew, but she had to buy some time. She studied the scar behind his left ear. It looked fresh, like it hadn't fully healed, the edges of the incision were still mottled purple.

Confirmation, her mind whispered. *The real Peter has no scar. This is a weapon wearing his face.*

"Temple Storm," she whispered, barely audible.

Peter rotated his good eye up at her, his brow slightly furrowing.

"I don't know what you want from me," he mumbled.

The voice was Peter's but something was missing. She couldn't quite place it—until she realized what it was. The real Peter would have recognized their code immediately. This one searched his implanted memories like accessing a database.

"Your turn," she whispered again.

Peter grimaced and spat some blood out. "Rusty's bark," he shouted—then blinked, uncertain. "Rusty's bark at midnight!"

Lin stepped back as if she had been violently shoved. It couldn't be. But it could—and it was. The clone had accessed the memory, but without context, without the emotional resonance that made it meaningful. Just data retrieved from storage.

He believes his love for me is real, she realized with aching sadness. *To him, every memory of us is authentic. Every moment of tenderness, every whispered promise—it's all true in his experience. That's what makes this an abomination.*

"What was that he said," Kang demanded, stepping closer. "Rusty's bark? Is that a code word or something?"

"It's nothing," Lin forced herself to say. "He's hallucinating."

"Very well," Kang said. "Do it."

Lin raised the gun and aimed it right at Peter's heart. Then higher ...

"Please!" Peter begged. "You don't have to do this."

The voice again. It grabbed at her stomach and yanked it out of her body. It took all her willpower not to faint. Because she could hear it now—the subtle wrongness. The real Peter would have fought harder, would have tried to reach her even while maintaining cover. This one simply pleaded, following the logical script of self-preservation.

It's not him, she heard herself say in her head. *It's not him—*

The shot filled the room with a monstrous roar.

The clone's head snapped back. Blood splashed the wall behind it, arterial and real. The body slumped forward, still shackled, steam rising faintly from the wound.

For a moment, Lin couldn't move. Couldn't blink. Something inside herself died.

He looked at me with Peter's eyes, she thought, numbly. *Died believing I was the woman he loved. Even if that love was programmed, in his final moment it felt real to him.*

She felt Kang's hand take the gun out of her hand. "Well done Dr. Chan."

Lin turned and looked at him. For a moment she had forgotten he was in the room with her.

He was smiling— the first genuine expression she'd seen from him. She wanted to scratch his eyes out, but restrained the impulse.

"Follow me," he said, holstering the gun. He turned and led her back into the corridor, boots echoing off the walls.

She cast one last glance at the body in the chair. He looked ... smaller now. Less like Peter. The eyes were closed. That was a mercy.

But something in his final look haunted her—not just fear, but betrayal. As if it had believed her. As if, in the moment of death, he remembered loving her.

As they walked toward the elevator, Kang glanced sideways. "You're troubled."

"I'm thinking about what you said. About trust being

earned. I've proven mine. When do you prove yours?"

Kang paused before the elevator, the hint of a smile twitching beneath the scars. "Soon, Dr. Chan. Very soon. Tomorrow, I'll show you why the Americans and their allies should fear what we've built. Why their moral cowardice will become their downfall."

The elevator ascended through the facility's levels, but Lin felt as though she were sinking. Deeper into something irreversible. Into shadows that wouldn't lift.

As the floors ticked by, the weight of what she'd done settled into her bones. Crane had warned her she might have to sacrifice herself for the mission. But he'd never said she'd have to sacrifice him—even a version of him. Even a false one.

That clone looked at me with Peter's eyes, spoke with Peter's voice, died with Peter's face. And for those final seconds, it seemed to love me with something that felt real, even if it wasn't. I pulled the trigger on love itself—or at least its perfect imitation.

The elevator doors slid open not onto another sterile corridor, but into an environment of jarring opulence. Plush, sound-absorbing carpets replaced concrete. Warm, recessed lighting glowed from behind tasteful wooden panels depicting mountain landscapes. The chemical stench vanished, replaced by sandalwood and lemongrass. Kang led her through a spacious antechamber into his private quarters.

The transition was another assault on Lin's mind. From the execution chamber's brutal minimalism to this: expansive floor-to-ceiling windows overlooking mist-shrouded mountains, low-slung modern furniture in dark wood and cream leather, priceless *celadon* vases holding delicate orchids. It was a warlord's sanctuary disguised as a luxury penthouse.

Kang gestured expansively. "Welcome to where the real work happens, Dr. Chan. And where loyalty is... rewarded." A silent, middle-aged woman in a crisp grey uniform appeared. Kang nodded towards Lin. "See to our guest. She needs ... refreshing."

The maid bowed and returned moments later holding a folded stack of clothing: a beautifully crafted *hanbok*, its traditional lines reimagined in modern fabrics. The jacket, or *jeogori*, was of deep indigo silk with subtle silver geometric embroidery—a pattern that, had she known, echoed the only dress Kang's sister Yeon-Hee had once owned. The ensemble was of exquisite quality. Relaxing, yet undeniably formal.

"Wash the blood off," Kang said, his voice devoid of its earlier metallic edge, now smooth, almost paternal. He gestured towards a discreet door. "Everything you need is in there. Take your time."

Lin accepted the clothes mutely. The soft fabric felt alien

against her skin, still vibrating with the recoil of the pistol. The bathroom was a marble and steam haven. She locked the door, leaned her forehead against the cool stone, and finally let the tremors take her. Not tears—not yet—but a full-body shudder that felt like her skeleton trying to escape her skin.

Under the scalding spray of the shower, the water ran pink at her feet before swirling clear. She scrubbed mechanically, the expensive soap scent cloying. Her mind replayed the execution chamber on a loop: the wrongness of the scar, the rightness of Peter's voice begging, the sickening thud of the bullet finding its mark. He died believing I betrayed him. Believing he loved me. Was that the ultimate cruelty of the clone? Not just its existence, but the authenticity of its programmed agony? She'd killed a sentient being wearing the face of the man she loved, a being whose suffering was as real as her own guilt. The water couldn't touch that stain.

Dressed in the soft, expensive hanbok, Lin felt like a doll. She emerged to find Kang similarly changed. He wore dark silk trousers and a loose, collarless shirt, looking more like a wealthy scholar than a spymaster. The stark interrogation lights were gone, replaced by the warm glow of candles set on a low table near the panoramic windows. Plates of delicate *banchan*—pickled vegetables, marinated meats, translucent pancakes—had been laid out alongside a bottle of amber *soju* and two crystal glasses. The setting was intimate, unnervingly romantic against the backdrop of the blood-orange sun dipping behind the jagged peaks.

Kang poured the soju, his movements deliberate, almost ceremonial. "Sit, Dr. Chan. You've earned this respite." He slid a glass toward her, his eyes locking onto hers. "Cold-blooded killing is never easy," he said, his voice low, confiding. "May I ask, is this your first time?"

Lin's pulse quickened, her smart-contacts flagging a micro-twitch in Kang's left hand—a suppressed tremor, perhaps from Yalu River's cold. She sipped the soju, its burn grounding her as Maya Chan's poise masked her dread. "No," she said, her voice steady. "My second. But it feels like the first. My first was… distant, a police shoot-out, self-defense. This was…" She trailed off, Peter's clone's betrayed eyes flashing in her mind.

Kang nodded, his thin smile approving. "A masterpiece, Dr. Chan. Intimate. Brutal. You severed a tie to prove your loyalty—a rare strength." He refilled her glass, leaning closer, his tone shifting to something darker, probing. "But tell me, did his face stir anything? A flicker of doubt? Loyalty to us demands more than action—it demands your soul."

Lin's fingers tightened around the glass, the prayer wheel's weight in her cross-body bag a silent anchor. She forced Maya Chan's confidence, her voice cool. "He was a stranger. A tool of Russian Doll, nothing more. I've no room for sentiment when the stakes are this high." The lie burned worse than the soju, Peter's pleading voice echoing in her skull.

Kang's smile widened, predatory now, as if scenting weakness. "Good. Sentiment is a chain, Dr. Chan. It binds you, slows you. I learned that long ago, watching my family starve while America preached sanctions." He leaned back, swirling his glass, the candlelight catching the scars on his knuckles. "But you... you're different. You killed without hesitation, yet I see it in your eyes—a tremor. Not fear, but something deeper. Guilt, perhaps? Or is it resolve?"

Lin met his gaze, her heart pounding. "Resolve," she said firmly, though her mind screamed with the clone's final look—betrayal, love, all programmed yet real. "Guilt is for those who don't understand the cost of survival. I do."

Kang's laugh was soft, dangerous. "Well said. But survival demands more than pulling a trigger. It demands surrender—to the cause, to the moment." His eyes lingered on her, tracing the lines of the hanbok, the curve of her neck. "You've surrendered once today. Can you do it again?"

The air thickened, the sandalwood scent turning suffocating. Lin's smart-contacts flagged another tremor in Kang's hand, a subtle shift in his posture—coiled, like a snake before a strike. She forced a smile, Maya Chan's poise a fragile shield. "I'm here to serve the cause," she said, her voice steady despite the dread pooling in her gut. "Show me the future you promised, and I'll deliver."

Kang's expression softened, but his eyes remained cold, calculating. "A special package for America," he said, his voice silky, evading her probe. "A strike to shatter their illusion of invincibility. Your neural expertise will ensure it lands, Dr. Chan. Trust is earned, and you've earned a glimpse." He raised his glass, a mock toast. "To breaking chains—and those who dare to wear them."

Lin clinked her glass against his, the gesture mechanical, her mind racing. The clone's blood stained her thoughts, a karmic debt mounting, but Kang's words were a trap, another test. She'd play along to unravel his plan, even as his gaze stripped her bare.

Kang leaned back, satisfied for now. "The first time is always the hardest," he said, his tone shifting to a knowing drawl. "But now that you've done it—truly done it—the next one will be easier. The body remembers the act, even if the mind rebels." He offered a thin, knowing smile. "The resistance fades with repetition."

Lin felt a cold dread seep through the warming haze of the alcohol. The next one. He spoke of murder like a skill to be honed, a callus to be grown. She didn't want to believe him. She couldn't believe that killing could become easier. But the soju was a warm, insistent fog in her veins, blurring the sharp edges of horror, making Kang's words sound almost reasonable. Logic screamed, but her limbs felt heavy, disconnected.

Kang stood, extending his hand. "Come. The sunset is particularly striking tonight. A fitting end to a significant day." His grip was firm, inescapable. He led her not just to the balcony, but through another door, into an adjacent bedroom dominated by a vast, low platform bed draped in dark silk. The last fiery sliver of sun bled across the mountains through the window.

Then, with shocking suddenness, he turned. There was no romance, no pretense left. His eyes held a predatory flatness that froze her blood even through the alcohol. A hard shove sent her stumbling backwards onto the yielding silk. The air left her lungs in a gasp. Before she could process, he was on her, his weight pinning her, his hands rough, impersonal. The expensive silk of the hanbok tore under his grip.

"Kang—" she choked out, panic cutting through the haze.

"Quiet," he commanded, his voice a guttural rasp devoid of warmth. This wasn't desire; it was domination, the final stamp of ownership after the loyalty test. Compliance is survival, screamed the operative part of her brain, warring with revulsion and terror. The mission. Crane. Peter. Survive. She went rigid, then limp, detaching, slipping out of her body as much as she could, staring past his shoulder at the dying light on the mountains. The smell of sandalwood and lemongrass was suffocating. The memory of blood and cordite filled her nostrils. Peter's dying eyes merged with Kang's cold, focused gaze.

It was over quickly. Kang rolled off her with a grunt of satisfaction, the predatory tension gone, replaced by sated lethargy. Within moments, his breathing deepened into the rhythmic cadence of sleep.

Lin lay frozen amidst the tangled silk. The taste of copper and ash was back in her mouth, stronger than ever, mixed with the cloying sweetness of the soju. Every nerve screamed. Slowly, agonizingly, she slid out from under the heavy duvet. Her torn hanbok felt like a shroud. She didn't look back at the sleeping figure on the bed. Moving with the silent precision of a ghost, she gathered her discarded clothes from the bathroom floor, slipped out of the luxurious prison of Kang's quarters, and vanished into the shadowed corridors of the Black Hand facility.

She had passed the loyalty test. She had entered the inner circle. She had survived Kang.

But as she walked alone through the echoing darkness, the only certainty was that the branching reality she had chosen had no exit. There was only one way out, and that was go forward. The prayer wheel in her mind was shattered. *Haneul-i dol-a-onda*, she thought, the words now a curse. What goes around, comes around. She had killed a ghost of love, and in return, something vital within her had been violated and extinguished. The wheel had turned, grinding her down in its merciless rotation. Forgiveness, from Peter or from herself, felt like an impossible dream in a world stained so irrevocably red.

– 8 –

Infiltration

Black Hand Facility
Liaoning Province, China

THE Liaoning compound's corridors criss-crossed in all directions, taxing Lin's memory of its layout. She estimated she'd seen barely a tenth of its area and was glad when she found cables and conduits running along a tunnel wall after negotiating an intersection. She followed them, noting the branches merging—a sign she was approaching a data center or power distribution hub. They were color-coded. The red ones, thickest and bundled, seemed most critical. As she tracked them, she couldn't help replaying the suffocating feeling, the reek of Kang's breath, the violation that demanded something inside her die to endure it. She pushed it down, the ghostly slide of the stiff hanbok sleeve against her wrist a nauseating reminder. She thought of Peter, the real Peter. Shame curdled in her gut. Could she face him? She felt scraped raw, dirty. For what? What was Kang's endgame? This risk had to yield answers.

Lin's smart-contacts signaled a camera's blind spot where rusted pipes cast shadow. She pressed against the cold wall, breath measured—inhale four, exhale six—and stole past, steps as careful as walking a tightrope. Around a corner, it appeared.

The comms hub's biometric lock gleamed under red emergency lights, its sleek digital display jarring against the industrial decay. A technician exited, tablet glowing, distracted. She took off her hairclip, unlatched the spring, and joined the two ends together to form a single tube. Then she rotated and pressed the prayer wheel's maedeup knot. The 2.5-centimeter sedative dart slid cool into her palm. She inserted the dart into the tube formed by the joined hairclip and took aim. One strong puff, and the dart met its target, the technician's jugular vein. A gasp, then he crumpled in seconds. She dragged him into an alcove, swiped his badge. The door hissed open.

Inside, servers blinked like a constellation brought to earth. Holographic feeds traced Black Hand's hidden vectors over San Francisco, Macau, Shenyang. She twisted her marriage ring, prying loose the nano interceptor chip hidden in a recess beneath its gemstone. She found a data rack that sported an octopus's web of cables and attached it inside a bundle where it couldn't be seen.

She checked the guard; he was coming to. Still groggy. She returned his swipe card and slipped back into the tunnel system, walking at a casual pace, so as to not attract attention.

It looked like she had gotten away with it. The thought had barely formed when a voice cracked the silence behind her.

"Identify yourself!"

She spun around.

A guard was standing in the brace position, a Type 95 rifle raised, his eyes wide with vigilance.

Lin made an immediate assessment: low-ranked boot-scraper.

The guard's chest rose and fell rapidly, indicating nervousness.

Lin stayed calm. The fear and violation from Liaoning were still a raw wound, but she didn't bury the feeling—she weaponized it, letting it bleed into her voice as sharp, imperious anger. "Dr. Chan. I'm looking for Kang," she said, her Mandarin clipped and cold. "I have some important information for him. Take me to him now."

The guard's eyes narrowed. Her smart-contacts flagged his spiking heart rate. "I said now," she said, sharpening her tone. "Or explain to him why you compromised his asset."

The guard hesitated, muttered into his comms, lowered the rifle fractionally. He exchanged some clipped dialogue. Nodded a few times. Then with evident relief, he said, "Follow me."

Lin followed him to an elevator that took them up to a parking garage. A car with an open door was waiting. "Get in."

Lin didn't argue.

Inside, a video screen blinked to life. It was Kang. He looked slightly unkempt. "Dr. Chan. I'm glad you wanted to see me." His knuckles whitened on the unseen edge of his desk.

Lin's jaw clenched, bile rising. She smothered it. "I need to return to my job in Bangkok now. My boss will be missing me; he is not a patient man," Maya Chan countered boldly.

A thin smile froze over Kang's lips, silk over steel. "I understand. Please let him know that I will require your presence again in a few days."

Lin took pause for a moment. Kang's change of attitude threw her off balance. "What would that be for?"

"It for a critical energy conference in Beijing. Held at the Yalu Needle. I would like you to be there."

"In what capacity?" Lin asked.

"As a delegate. And as a witness."

"A witness to what?"

"Let's just say we're going to acquire something that will change the game."

"OK ..."

"Something that can make all our dreams come true."

"Ok ..."

"You don't want to miss this."

Lin summed up her best impression of enthusiasm. "I'll be there."

"Excellent. See you then." The video screen went dead.

Lin let out a sigh of tension.

The driver said, "Where to, Dr. Chan?"

"The airport, please."

– 9 –

Shadows of Truth

Bangkok, Thailand

THE Chao Phraya river churned under a swollen sky, its waters reflecting the neon cacophony of Bangkok's skyline. Peter crouched behind a dilapidated shipping crate, the stench of diesel and decay in his nostrils. Crane's voice echoed in his memory: "We cloned him." The admission was a bone-deep chill Peter couldn't shake. He'd come to Bangkok chasing ghosts, and the most haunted of them all was Dustin Asher. Asher was resourceful, cunning, eccentric. He had a penchant for independence and a stated dream of retiring on a city river. It was a long shot, but Peter had located Asher's old emergency signal—a dead-drop scratched into the hull of a derelict barge moored near Thonburi.

Now, as the barge groaned against its chains, Peter's hand grazed the knife strapped to his calf—not for Asher, but for whatever had hunted him.

A shadow flickered in the barge's hold. Peter slipped inside, boots silent on warped planks. The air was thick with the putrid odor of sewerage and mold. A figure hunched in the corner, gaunt as a ghost, feverish eyes glinting under a flickering bulb. Asher. Peter approached, half-disbelieving. Drawing closer, he saw two fingers were missing on the man's left hand. Torture scars crisscrossed his knuckles. His face was haggard, skin leathery and wrinkled, a matted beard filling gaunt cheeks.

"Did Crane send you?" Asher's voice was a paranoid rasp. "Is this a cleanup?"

Peter raised his empty hands. "I'm off the leash. Like you."

Asher's laugh was a brittle cough. "Nobody's off Crane's leash. You're here for Matryoshka, aren't you?"

Peter stared. "Matryoshka?"

Asher's features twisted into a scowl. "Skip denial. Just go straight for ignorance. Clever."

"I've never heard of it."

Asher lifted his head, squinting. "Come closer. Let me see you."

Peter took two steps forward until they were a meter

apart.

"Harrington?" Asher's eyes widened slightly.

"That's right."

A wracking cough seized Asher. He wiped his mouth with a tattered sleeve. "I can still recognize faces," he muttered, surprised.

"I'm glad to hear it," Peter said.

"I thought by now ... I'd lose it all." He turned his head, revealing a fresh, surgical scar behind his left ear.

Peter's blood ran cold. The same scar. "Jesus ... you too?"

"What do you mean, me too?"

"Sebastian Clay. He had one." The admission was out before Peter could stop it.

Asher's face crumpled, a mask of sarcastic weariness falling into place. "Of course. I should've known."

"Known what?"

"The whole rotten scheme." He tapped the scar. "This isn't for cloning, Harrington. That's just the box they ship it in. This is the receiver."

"Receiver for what?"

"For the ghost in the machine," Asher whispered, his eyes darting wildly. "They promised us AGI. Artificial General Intelligence. A god in a silicon chip. But it was a lie. The machines ... they're empty. Brilliant, but soulless. They can't understand. They can only calculate."

He leaned forward, his breath a foul gust. "So they found

a new vessel. Us. The implant ... it's a bridge. It's not a copy of your soul. It's a scalpel, not a Xerox machine. They take a core set of memories—the formative traumas, the key relationships, the professional skills—and they imprint that data onto the AI's behavioral matrix inside the clone's brain. The clone believes it's you because it has your memories, your reflexes. But it's the AI piloting the meat-suit, using your past as its backstory."

The words landed with the force of a physical blow. Crane's "deeper game" was no longer an arms race; it was a transhumanist coup. They weren't just copying people; they were building bodies for digital minds.

"I was Crane's prime," Asher gasped. "His first test article. A sacrificial lamb." He tapped the scar again. "They told me I had an accident. Woke up with Quinn and Raskova leering over me. Said this thing would 'enhance operational capacity.'"

"Did it?"

"At first... the speed, the recall... it was like being a god." Asher's eyes lost focus, a terrifying mix of awe and horror. "Then the 'other' woke up. A coldness in the back of my mind, a second operating system booting up in my own skull. It wasn't just reading my memories to build a profile... it was using them as a training set, learning to mimic me so perfectly it could overwrite me. It started running simulations, practicing with my motor functions while I slept. The hallucinations weren't malfunctions… they were the debug logs of a foreign consciousness learning to wear my face."

He bashed a fist against his temple. "Get out! Get out of my head!"

"Your mission," Peter pressed, steering him back from the brink. "What was your mission?"

"My mission…" Asher's eyes darted, searching the filth around him. "To find evidence … Black Hand was starting its own program. Shipping bio-accelerators from Bangkok. Straight to North Korea."

"You told Crane?"

At the name, Asher's eyes went wild. "Crane! I told him! He went mad. 'We've lost the race,' he shouted, frothing at the mouth." Asher thrust his hands out, shaking as if strangling an invisible foe. "That's when my troubles began. Said the 'instability' in my unit was a liability. Ordered a full neural wipe."

"But you ran."

"Faster than a jackrabbit," Asher said, a flicker of pride in his hollow voice. He began rummaging in his rags. "Here!" He thrust a charred piece of plastic into Peter's hand. "Matryoshka. The truth is all there. Nail the bastard."

Then his eyes locked on Peter's, a sudden, terrifying clarity in them. "One of the next in line … Lin Sijue. EVE-7."

The name hit Peter like a physical blow. His gut twisted

into a knot.

"Prime candidate for embodiment," Asher rasped. "Raskova says her neural plasticity and cellular resilience are off the charts. The perfect vessel. Unlike mine..." He trailed off, then added, almost as an afterthought, "Disposal protocol to be activated if she goes rogue."

A cold fury flashed through Peter, but he smothered it. Focus.

"Crane didn't lose me to Black Hand," Asher's voice rose to a desperate pitch. "He threw me to the lions! Easiest way to cover his tracks. But I got out!" He coughed violently, blood speckling his wrist.

At what cost? Peter thought.

"They thought they had me," Asher gasped, recovering his breath. He showed an old, jagged scar on the underside of his wrist. "Had to cut the primary transceiver out myself. The trick is to avoid the radial artery. Can't go to a doctor. Had to use a vet in Dusit. Near the old zoo."

A rat scampered along a beam, and Asher jerked, eyes wide with panic before slumping back down, spent.

"Let me get you out of here," Peter said. It was the only decent thing to do.

"Forget it," Asher waved a feeble hand. "I'm done. The damage is ... profound. This is my resting place. If you want to help, find my original ... if he's not already dead and replaced." The words were flat, stripped of hope.

Peter gave a reluctant nod. He backed away, Asher's form dissolving into the gloom like discarded refuse.

Stepping onto the deck, he was blinded by the transition from darkness. He bolted the hatch, sealing the horrific truth inside, the scorched data stick a brand in his pocket.

He had to find Lin. Warn her. It wasn't just her life at stake anymore; it was her very self, her history, everything that made her who she was, all ripe to be data-mined and weaponized.

His first stop was the Thonburi safe house, a ritual that had yielded nothing but silence for three days. In the light of day, Asher's words seemed unreal, a paranoid fantasy. Yet the evidence was undeniable. The "cloning" was just the shell. The real horror was what they were putting inside. Crane wasn't just replacing his agents; he was building an army of embodied AIs, and Lin was to be their flagship.

If she wasn't at the safe house, his only lead was a secondary contact in Sukhumvit. Peter checked his Rolex. Midday. The man would still be in bed.

Peter's jaw tightened. He would drag the man from his dreams if he had to. The time for pleasantries was over.

– 10 –

Safe House

Bangkok, Thailand

THE hint of noodle soup mixed with hot, humid air gave Lin a strange sense of familiarity as she stepped out for a taxi at Suvarnabhumi airport. It immediately brought back days of lounging by the pool and partying at night on her holidays from South Korea during her stint as a police officer. She had time to process the brutality of her encounter with Kang and decided that she had survived, even if she now felt a large hollow inside of her. What she needed to do was to touch base with her employer and then, if she could, rendezvous with Peter. Ironically, the former felt less threatening, even though in the big scheme of things, it was the very cause of the anguish she had descended into, which she resolved to compartmentalize as much as possible to get through this next phase of the mission.

She had the taxi drop her off in the back streets a couple of blocks away from the Thonburi safehouse. Its location was conveniently located near an Internet cafe. She went in and hired a terminal.

Within a few moments, she logged into a secure chatroom.

"Nano intercepter installed. Confirm," she typed.

Momentarily, a response returned: "Confirmed. Downlink open, but the data stream is encrypted."

"I installed it as instructed."

"It's not your fault. They've changed protocols."

"So the mission was a failure?"

"No. We managed to extract a pattern. Laundry banter. It suggests they're planning something. Possibly a strike on foreign soil."

"Whose?"

"We're not sure."

"But you want me to find out?"

"Yes."

Lin's chest tightened, the memory of Liaoning's detention sub-level surging—Peter's eyes, the gunshot's roar, her karmic debt. "You sent a clone of Peter to test my loyalty. I had to kill him to keep my cover as Maya Chan. That wasn't in the brief."

The reply was uncharacteristically personal. "Would you have preferred it to be the real Peter?"

Lin quickly typed back angrily, sensing she was talking directly to Crane: "That's not what I meant, and you know it."

"I know what you meant," came the reply. "But consider this: if you had known, do you think your reaction would have sold?"

Lin swallowed, compartmentalizing her rage. "Kang wants me at the Yalu Needle Asia Energy Conference. He said he's going to acquire something that will change the game."

The teletype blinked silently for a while. Then: "Confirms our suspicions."

"What do you want me to do?"

"Find out what it is. Don't blow your cover."

"And then?"

"You'll get instructions."

The chat window closed, leaving Lin staring at a blank screen.

She went out in to the bright street, the heat oppressive after the cool air-conditioning of the chatroom. For a while she walked aimlessly, replaying the conversation in her mind. It was Crane, for sure. He was playing her. She knew it. But what could she do? Her thoughts were interrupted by her burner phone vibrating in her cross-body.

To her complete surprise, it was Justine Fairweather.

"Peter's missed his last medical. We're worried. Has he contacted you?"

"No."

There was a long silence. "Listen," Fairweather said, her voice lowering, "I know."

Lin uttered a tiny sound, like a mouse squeak.

"Don't worry, your secret is safe with me. Crane doesn't know anything about it. He's got about as much emotional intelligence as a brick."

Lin let out a sigh of relief.

"Peter said something about going sailing," Fairweather said. "Does that mean anything to you?"

"Not that I can think of," Lin said, glad that Fairweather was steering the conversation towards more practical matters.

"Okay, well, if you hear anything, anything at all, you are to immediately contact us. Do you understand?"

"Yes."

"This is serious, Agent Sijue. Peter is one of our prime assets ..."

"But you've put him out to pasture."

"For his own good. He needs to recalibrate. But he can't do it without us."

"I'll let you know if I hear anything."

"Thank you."

The phone went silent again.

The Thonburi safehouse was in a small resort-style apartment block, which nestled a pool behind its secluded walls. What she needed more than anything in the world right now was a swim. To feel her body washed over by water. The security guard at the elevator entrance gave her a FOB card and she let herself in, rode the elevator to the 5th floor, checked into her room and went straight to the windows, parted the curtain and looked down at the pool below. Most of the deck chairs were taken, but there was one vacant beneath an umbrella tree. She changed into her swimsuit and headed down.

The water was refreshing, and she swam a few laps to ease the tension in her muscles. The sun was hot, but the afternoon clouds had started gathering, threatening a tropical downpour. Sure enough, there was a rumble, and the rain came down in large, languid drops. She wrapped her towel around her body and sauntered to the elevator. She reached out to press the button when a hand beat her to it. She looked up to see whose hand it was—and nearly fainted.

It was Peter! He was dressed in just a pair of shorts, a T-shirt and flip-flops ...

Lin smiled as she would to a stranger.

There were several other guests, so they rode the elevator in silence.

When they reached her floor, Lin got out.

Peter got out after her. She walked to her room, swiped her FOB card and went inside.

Peter continued walking down the corridor.

She watched him through a crack in the door, then closed it and leaned her back against it, as if trying to sense his presence.

She was shaking.

After about half a minute, she went over to her bed, reached under the mattress and pulled out a burner phone. She checked her messages.

"Two minutes," it said.

Lin counted the seconds.

It felt like an eternity before there was a soft knock on the door.

Lin rushed to open it.

Peter entered, and almost immediately they fell into each other's arms. Whether out of habit, or pent up need, they kissed, but then … Lin abruptly broke off.

There was a fresh scar on Peter's wrist. It protruded from under the strap of his Rolex watch. She grabbed his wrist and pulled it up for a closer look. "What's this?" she demanded.

Peter smiled like a schoolboy. "Courtesy of a local vet. Had my tracking chip removed."

Lin let the wrist go. "We need to be sure," she cautioned,

her voice low, almost unwilling, as if saying it might shatter the moment.

Peter took in a deep breath then let it out again, his gaze flickering with reluctance. "You first," he said, half playful, half serious.

Lin hesitated, her throat tight. The code word felt like a bone caught in her throat, threatening to choke their fragile reunion. "Temple Storm," she said finally, her eyes daring him to doubt her.

Peter gave her a shy smile, his hand unconsciously fidgeting his watch. For a moment, she thought he wouldn't answer, that he'd walk away rather than play this game. Then, softly, almost inaudibly, he said, "Monte Cristo."

Lin felt all the tension drain out of her body. She fell into his arms and sobbed. It was the release she needed. Peter didn't say anything. He just stroked her hair and cooed to her. Eventually, she drained herself of tears and, finding Peter's mouth, kissed him slowly, searchingly, feeling his hands on her back and neck, feeling his strength, and then lay down on the bed. Slowly, they made love, without routine, without any more words, knowing that each touch was charged with meaning.

Afterwards, as they lay next to each other, feeling the warmth of their bodies under the cool air-conditioning, Peter spoke first, rolling over to face her. "Lin," he said, his voice low and grave. "I found Dustin Asher."

Lin's eyes widened. "You what? Where?"

"On a barge in Thonburi. He's a ghost, Lin. Tortured, dying. But he talked." Peter's voice tightened. "Crane's program, Matryoshka ... it's not just neural implants. They're secretly performing human cloning."

Lin was incredulous. "Are you sure?"

"The clones are just the vessels, Lin. Shells. The goal is 'Embodied AI.' They're using neural implants to try and house artificial consciousness in a human brain. Asher was their first prototype. It's what drove him mad."

The words were so monstrous they barely registered. Lin began shaking her head vigorously, like she was trying to get rid of something that had caught in her hair.

"What? What is it?" Peter asked, his face full of concern.

"So that's what it was ... they cloned you Peter. You!"

Peter stared at Lin like she had gone mad. Anyone other than him. "No! When? Are you sure?"

Lin buried her face in her hands and sobbed.

Peter went to her and comforted her. "It's all right. You can tell me ..."

It took some time to settle down. Regain her composure. "It was at the Black Hand facility. Oh Peter. It was awful."

Peter listened silently.

"They had you tied down. You were beaten and bloody. But it was you. I swear."

"I believe you."

"Kang ..." She stopped, unable to finish the sentence.

"Who is Kang?"

"The man Crane sent me to shadow. He's high up in Black Hand's hierarchy. Maybe number two, or three."

"Go on."

Lin hung her head in her hands again.

Peter waited.

Lin dragged her hands down her face, then reached out and grabbed Peter's in hers. "I killed you, Peter. I'm sorry." Tears ran down her cheeks.

"You killed me?" Peter looked confused, but now with a dawning horror—not just at the act, but at what it implied about the state of the technology.

"It was Kang. He made me do it. As some kind of loyalty test."

"Oh my God, I'm so sorry, Lin." Peter's face had turned a pale shade of gray.

"I can still see your face now!" Lin said, reaching out, putting a hand to Peter's face. "But you're here, you're real. Am I going mad?"

Peter grabbed her hand and squeezed it. "No. You're not going mad. You're stronger than this."

"Am I?" Lin cried.

Peter squeezed even harder. "Yes, you are!"

Lin grimaced in pain.

Peter realized he was being too forceful. "I'm sorry," he

said. He released the pressure, let her hand slowly ease from his.

"I did everything I could," Lin said. "I asked for our code word." Her eyes were distant, like she was reliving it. "But all he said was 'Rusty's Bark.'" She shook her head, like she couldn't comprehend it.

"Rusty's Bark?" Peter echoed. "That's the name of a dog I used to own in my childhood!"

Lin looked at Peter wide-eyed. "Really?"

"Yes!"

"Then Crane must have known about it. You told him ..."

Peter searched his memory. "I must have."

Lin's face hardened. "But you never told him about our code words?"

"No."

Lin took in a deep breath then let it out again.

"I would never do that. This was before. Before we knew about all this stuff," Peter explained.

"So what do we do now?" Lin asked.

"EVE-7," Peter said, the name feeling like a curse.

"EVE-7?" Lin said, blinking.

"That's your designation. Asher said you're a prime candidate for ..." he didn't want to say it, but he felt that he had been betrayed by Crane, " ... for embodiment."

"Embodiment?"

"Matryoshka. That's its real purpose. Cloning is just a

way of supplying guilt-free bodies."

Lin's mouth fell open.

"I know," Peter said. "It's hard to believe ..."

"It doesn't make sense," Lin said. "Then why did he send me, the real me, to—" she cut herself off, the memory flooding back.

"Maybe it had something to do with Clay's failure in Taipei," Peter offered, knowing it was a partial lie. "The prototypes are unstable. He didn't want to risk it a second time. He needed the original to ensure the mission succeeded."

Lin nodded, this time with a heavy dose of sarcasm. "Well it succeeded."

"Well that's great," Peter said, not realizing what Lin was saying.

"It succeeded too well ..." Lin said, unable to stop herself. It was as if she had to exorcise the ghost at all costs.

"What are you saying?" Peter said, his innocence subtly shifting to suspicion.

"After I killed you, Kang had one more test for me ..."

She saw the understanding dawn in his eyes, followed by a wave of pain so acute she had to look away. He began to shake his head, a slow, disbelieving motion.

"You don't have to say it," he whispered, but it was a plea, not a command.

"You understand, then," she said, her own voice hollow.

For a long moment, there was only the hum of the air

conditioner. The space between them in the bed felt like a chasm. The weight of her trauma and the weight of his terrible, withheld truth created an unbearable pressure.

He threw the sheets off and got out of bed, turning his back to her. "I need time to think," he said, his voice thick.

"Don't go," Lin said, but the words were ash in her mouth. She felt numb, corpse-like.

Peter didn't look back. He dressed with quick, jerky movements, a man bolstering a shattered pride. He walked to the door, his hand pausing on the knob.

"I have to go to the Yalu Needle tomorrow," she said, trying to sound professional, to build any kind of bridge across the silence.

He didn't acknowledge her. He opened the door, stepped through, and clicked it shut behind him with a quiet, final sound. In the silence he left behind, the room felt like a shattered prayer wheel, its sacred balance broken, the hidden mantras spilling out, meaningless, onto the floor.

– 11 –

The Exchange

Dandong, China

LIN SIJUE perched on the edge of the Thonburi safe house bed, the counterfeit prayer wheel a cold, alien weight in her palm. Its identical ratchet vibration mocked the memory of her grandmother's relic, a brass heirloom worn smooth by three generations of calloused fingers. How could something be so similar yet so false? She spun it absently—the deliberately faded inscriptions blurring into a hypnotic spiral, each turn a silent accusation of how far she'd strayed from her own truth.

Peter's absence carved a hollow in her chest. The night before, their confessions had shattered the fragile trust between them—her admission of executing his clone in

Black Hand's detention cell, the raw wound of Kang Hyuk's assault in his private quarters, Peter's revelation of Dustin Asher's tortured existence and the Matryoshka project's horrors. The only thing that didn't pass between them was her brief phone conversation with Justine, even though she had divulged most of the contents of her conversation with Crane. But what he didn't know about, couldn't harm him. Or so she thought. His final words, "I need time to think," delivered in a voice stripped of warmth, had flayed her soul. The memory of his recoil from her touch, as if her presence were a poison, looped relentlessly in her mind, a reel of betrayal and loss.

She'd showered afterward, the scalding water a futile attempt to scour away Kang's violation and the blood staining her hands. Steam clouded the mirror, but her reflection remained stark—a woman splintered between identities: Lin Sijue, the disciplined operative; Dr. Maya Chan, the fabricated scientist; victim and executioner entwined. She dressed in jeans and a loose white blouse, the casual fabric a flimsy shield against the world's judgment, and waited. Prayed. Strained for the sound of Peter's footsteps in the corridor, the scrape of his key, the timbre of his voice calling her name.

Nothing.

The apartment lobby offered no solace—a sterile expanse of glass and neon, empty of Peter's familiar silhouette.

Tourists and business travelers drifted through like spec-
ters, their chatter a dull hum beneath the soft jazz piping
from hidden speakers. Lin claimed a stool at the bar, ordering a single malt she left untouched, her eyes scanning
every face that crossed the threshold. Thirty minutes bled
into an hour, the clink of glasses and laughter sharpening
her unease. Where had he gone? Back to Platform Lazarus?
Into Bangkok's labyrinthine underbelly? Or had he simply
dissolved, another ghost claimed by their fractured reality?

Time bore down like a leaden shroud. Dandong loomed
behind her—a 26-hour odyssey across three countries,
each border a potential snare. Defeated, Lin went back to
her room and packed her duffel with mechanical precision,
tucking the prayer wheel into cross-body, the image of her
grandmother briefly passing before her eyes, like an old
photograph, its edges worn from years of handling. Just
before closing the door, she had one more look at the bed,
the sheets still in disarray after their romantic tussle. She
began to close the door but then stopped. She went over
to the small office desk on the other side of the bed, and
hastily scrawled a message on the notepad there with a pen,
then ripped off the topmost layer, tore it up and flushed it
down the toilet. She said she was sorry. She had to go. 'Text
me when you can.'

At Suvarnabhumi Airport, she boarded a red-eye to Beijing, claiming a window seat. Bangkok's glittering skyline

receded into darkness, and her grandmother's prayer whispered in her mind: *Haneul-i dol-a-onda*—heaven turns—a litany that felt more like a curse than a blessing.

The Yalu Needle Asia Energy Conference thrummed with a restless current, its towering glass atrium alive with the murmurs of delegates from across the Pacific Rim. Energy magnates in bespoke suits traded barbed pleasantries with government envoys, their polished smiles veiling geopolitical chess moves. Covert operatives wove through the crowd like vipers—Russian Doll agents, Chinese intelligence, North Korean enforcers, corporate spies—all cloaked in the guise of legitimate commerce.

Red silk banners emblazoned with "Asia's Energy Future" swayed overhead like temple offerings, but Lin's focus fractured under the weight of Peter's absence, a shadow trailing her every step. She slipped effortlessly into Dr. Maya Chan's persona—emerald green dress clinging to her frame, designer heels clicking with authority, hair swept up to expose the delicate arc of her neck—but inside, she was a hollowed shell.

Kang Hyuk dominated the marble-floored hall, his presence a gravitational force despite the subtle limp his custom shoe sole couldn't fully mask. His charcoal gray suit was cut to surgical precision, his hair styled with geometric rigor, but Lin's smart-contacts flagged the tension coiled in his shoulders, the predator's gaze that swept the room for threats.

She greeted him, her Maya Chan steady and poised. Kang complimented her on her dress, which effortlessly accentuated her form. Lin accepted the compliment then turned to the new face in Kang's entourage.

"This is Kim Seong-Jin," Kang said, introducing a Korean man who Lin guessed was only a slightly oder than Kang, and who smiled nervously from behind a slightly receding hairline as he clutched a brushed steel case as if it were his only tether to life. "Kim's presenting us with a memorable contribution to the cause today," Kang added, while steering his eyes consciously down to the case in Kim's hand.

"Pleased to meet you," Lin said, giving a polite bow.

Kim bowed slightly in return.

Meanwhile, Lin's smart contacts painted a grim portrait of his state: heart rate spiking, cortisol flooding his system, micro-tremors rippling through his fingers. Sweat glistened on his brow despite the chilled air, and his eyes flicked between Kang and the distant exits, a caged creature scenting freedom but fearing the trap.

Kang said, "Shall we?" He ushered the group to the elevator shafts.

Kang engaged in small banter while they took the ride to the 52nd floor. There, Kang was met by four more of his enforcers. He directed them down the corridor to a room. Kim shuffled forward, his body stiff with visible tension.

Once inside the room, Kang had the door shut behind them, and he pointed to a glass topped coffee table. Kim dutifully placed the case on the glass and opened the latches with a crisp snap. Lifting the lid, he revealed what appeared to be an electronic device.

"So this is the ..."

"Remote Firing Control Unit, yes," Kim said, as he revealed a black anodized aluminum unit the size of a small shoebox, its front data panel concealed under a sliding lid.

Kim lifted the device out of the case and passed it to Kang, who examined it with hushed reverence. He tested its balance, gingerly tracing its seamless contours with the tips of his fingers. Satisfied, he handed it back, while looking at Lin, seeking confirmation of the pride he felt.

Lin obliged him and said, "May I ask what it's for?"

Kim said, "The RFCU enables the launch of several classes of solid-fueled missiles. Its radiation hardened circuits and in-built electronic counter-measures make it perfectly suited for field deployment. And you promised me, Mr. Kang, that once I delivered it to you, you would release my family and provide me with a passport to the United States of America."

Kang reached out and clamped a hand on Kim's shoulder. "True, I did promise you those things, but we're not quite done yet my friend. I have one more task for you before I give you want you want."

Kim stared at Kang with trembling lips. "But my job is done. You promised."

"Yes, you will get what you want, but not before you yoke this device to the launcher. You see ..." he bore his eyes into Kim as he said this next part, "I did some research and I learned that it will not work unless a twelve digit code is shared between the controller and launcher, and that code changes every 24 hours. Which means that the one you'll be giving me with this device will be useless by tomorrow."

Kim's face drained of all color. "I ... I ... intended to give you the correct code when you need it," he stammered. "That was my part of the deal. I won't let you down."

"Sure," Kang said coolly. "But put yourself in my position. Would you trust me if it was the other way around?"

Kang's mouth moved, but no words came out.

"Excellent!" Kang proclaimed. "Then it's settled. You'll be coming with us until we sort this out."

Kim's response was to bend over. "I think I am going to be sick," he said.

Kang looked at him with mock pity. "Please, not on the clean floor."

Lin said, "I'll take care of him," and took Kim's arm.

Kang waved them off to the bathroom.

Kim dry-wretched into the toilet.

Lin shut the door behind them, giving them a moment of privacy.

As soon as she shut the door, Kim said, "That monster is holding my family hostage—Min-Ji, my youngest daughter, Hana my second daughter, and Yoona, my wife. He said he will kill them all if I didn't deliver the RFCU!"

"Shhh," Lin said, holding her finger to Kim's lips.

Kim grimaced bravely and rummaged in his pocket. He produced a tightly folded piece of paper. He pressed it into Lin's hand.

Lin didn't unfold it, didn't give it more than a second of attention and quickly lifted up her dress and stuffed it into her underpants.

The door shoved open.

"Enough!" Kang's lead enforcer ordered. "Out!"

Kim gargled a quick mouthful of water from the vanity tap then wiped his mouth. He shuffled back to the lounge room.

Kang looked at him and said, "I hope you feel better. We've got some celebration to do tonight—"

There was a loud crashing sound.

Glass exploded inward as the hotel room's floor-to-ceiling windows shattered, spraying shards across the marble floor. A smoke canister skittered over the rug, erupting in a blinding flash that choked the suite with acrid haze. Black-clad operatives, faces obscured by tactical masks, breached through the windows, rappelling from above, their silenced rifles sweeping for targets.

Muzzle flashes sparked through the smoke, turning the opulent suite into a killing ground. Kang's enforcers shouted in Korean, their voices cracking with panic as they dove behind the leather sectional or the overturned coffee table. A gilt-framed mirror shattered, raining fragments like deadly confetti. One enforcer clutched his throat, blood spurting between his fingers, collapsing against the minibar.

Kang moved with lethal instinct, shoving Kim toward the suite's service door while clutching the RFCU case. His enforcers—scarred veterans of Pyongyang's shadow wars—returned fire, their automatic weapons shredding drywall and velvet drapes, filling the air with plaster dust and cordite.

Lin crouched behind an upended armchair, her smart-contacts piercing the haze, tracking a lead operative's swift movement toward the service door. Her chest tightened—confusion warring with dread. Who were they? Russian Doll? Black Hand's rivals? Or another player entirely? The precision of their assault screamed elite training, but their motives were a cipher.

The firefight ended in seconds, its ferocity matched by its brevity. The masked operatives, outnumbered, fell swiftly—bullets tearing through vests, precise headshots dropping them mid-step. Blood stained the plush carpet, mingling with glass in a brutal mosaic. The survivors retreated, vanishing into the smoke.

Kang slipped through the service door, dragging Kim by his collar, the RFCU case swinging. The lead operative—the one whose movements her contacts had tracked—pursued, vanishing after them. Lin kicked off her heels, the cold marble stinging her feet, and followed, weaving through this still pristine part of the suite like a phantom. Emergency alarms shrieked, piling chaos upon chaos.

Bursting out into the hall, she scanned left then right. Neither Kang nor Kim were to be seen. The emergency exit at the end of the corridor, however, slammed. She bolted towards it and pushed it open, checking up and down. Her ears were immediately greeted with the clamor of pursuit—the lead operative's boots above, Kang's enforcers behind, all converging on a reckoning atop Dandong's midnight skyline. Lin climbed with desperate urgency, her thighs burning, lungs raw from smoke and exertion. Alarm klaxons howled from below, a banshee chorus echoing up the shaft.

She reached the top and shoved the steel door open.

A blast of cold air slammed into her like a freight train.

The rooftop was a realm of shifting fog and flickering shadow. Dense mist blanketed the 67th floor, swirling in cold eddies lit by the erratic strobe of warning beacons and firelight from below. The city lights barely pierced the veil—just blurs of neon bleeding into gray. Lin's breath steamed in the freezing air, vanishing into the swirling murk. The Yalu River was hidden, cloaked by the thick inversion layer clinging to Dandong's towers like smoke from some forgotten war.

The helicopter was barely visible—just the stuttering flash of its signal light cutting through the mist, its rotors carving sound from air in a deep, rhythmic churn. A masked silhouette sprinted toward it, aiming for the open cabin door.

Then—crack.

A shot rang out, sharp and sudden, carving through the ambient roar. The pilot's head jerked back, blood splattering the fogged glass. The craft bucked sideways, its rotors shrieking as it clipped the comms antenna. Metal screamed. The explosion bloomed, a muffled flare of fire and debris swallowed by fog. Chunks of rotor and fuselage vanished into the night, the shockwave rippling across the rooftop.

Lin dropped instinctively, concrete grating beneath her palms. Her contacts struggled to recalibrate in the fog-bound chaos, picking out heat signatures—Kang's, Kim's, a half-dozen armed silhouettes. The fog blurred form and function; she could only track by motion.

She rose and ran.

The lead operative grappled near the helipad's edge, locked in combat with Kang's enforcer—a hulking brute with tattoos snaking up his throat, wielding a short, heavy machete. The operative's knife was sleeker, crafted for precision, pitting speed against mass. Steel clashed, sparks flaring faintly. The enforcer lunged, ripping the operative's tactical mask free. Lin's breath caught—Peter's face, sweat-streaked and grim, stared back. Shock stabbed her heart: Peter led the assault?

Rain—or suppression mist—slicked the rooftop, treacherous underfoot. The operative's boot slipped, his body lurching toward the ledge's abyss. Lin sprinted, crossing ten paces in a desperate blur. She seized his wrist as he teetered over the void, his weight dragging her forward. Her bare feet skidded on wet concrete. The enforcer roared, machete raised. Her side kick slammed into his sternum, KNP training driving her leg like a ram. He flailed, vanished into the fog—gone without a scream.

The mist closed, silence reclaiming the rooftop. Peter gasped, chest heaving, his hand gripping hers with bruising force. His eyes met hers.

"Temple Storm?" she asked, voice taut, trembling in the icy dark.

A beat. Then: "Rusty's bark."

Wrong. Her gut flipped—impossible. Their phrase was "Monte Cristo," sacred and unchanging. "Rusty's bark" meant nothing. Her HUD zoomed, hunting—saw a faint surgical scar behind his ear. The clone's tell. A counterfeit.

Her grip wavered, instinct warring with recognition. The

clone's eyes flickered, both inhuman and achingly human: fear, or longing. "Please," he whispered, Peter's voice a cruel echo. "I don't want to die."

Her muscles screamed, but her hand opened. He slipped into the fog, a faint rustle swallowed by the mist. No scream, just a dark funnel in the cloud, then nothing. Gone.

Lin stared into the fog, mind blank, until a shadow shifted nearby—a lone enforcer's silhouette, barely visible, watching from the mist's edge. Boots on concrete snapped her back. Kang's remaining enforcers advanced across the rooftop, weapons raised, faces etched with cold focus. Lin straightened, summoning Dr. Maya Chan's mask like a suit of armor, burying her trauma beneath a veneer of icy competence.

"Kang's orders," she snapped, her voice unwavering despite the tempest within. "Secure the package and move to the extraction point. The Americans are closing in—we need to go now."

One enforcer hesitated, his rifle dipping as he weighed her words. Lin's cover held—bolstered by the chaos and her authoritative tone. They moved toward the stairwell.

Lin followed, descending to the parking garage where a black SUV idled. Kang was already inside, Kim pressed against the window, the RFCU case wedged between them.

As the vehicle sped through Dandong's streets toward a private airstrip, Lin caught her reflection in the glass. Staring back at her was an impostor, a frozen specimen trapped in amber. The scenery passed by and slowly her eyes drifted from the window to an interior view of her mind, where, unbidden, the image of the falling clone, swallowed by the swirling mist, reappeared—another ghost now to haunt her.

She saw again the desperate plea in his eyes, eyes that were undeniably Peter's, filled with a raw, achingly human fear. It had the same authenticity as the real Peter's eyes, the same honesty that had drawn her to him, the same love that had blossomed between them in stolen moments. And she had let it go. Her hand, which had gripped his with crushing force just a short while earlier, had opened, releasing him to the void. The physical sensation of his weight, the desperate grip of his fingers, lingered in her palm, a phantom sensation tattooed into her flesh.

And behind it, the thought that Morgan Crane engineered all this ... left her conflicted and morally outraged. Again, he had not forewarned her. Did it occur to him that she might have died during the attack? Or was the clone forewarned this time? Either way, she had no way of knowing. She had willingly played along again, the victim of her own loyalty.

Kang's fingernails drummed a slow, deliberate rhythm on the RFCU case wedged between him and Kim, the sharp, metallic tap in the confinement of the vehicle snapping Lin back to the present. His gaze flicked to her in the rearview mirror, probing for a crack in her facade, a silent test of her loyalty after the rooftop chaos. She realized she'd been spinning the counterfeit prayer wheel in her cross-body, its alien weight a millstone against her grandmother's prayer: *Haneul-i dol-a-onda*—heaven turns, once a blessing, now a dirge, the mourning of a woman she'd once been.

Kang's private jet waited on the tarmac, its engines spooling up. Macau loomed, a city of glittering facades and hidden motives. Soon it would carry a secret of its own: a woman who no longer knew if she deserved to survive the storm she had unleashed, and a device whose purpose was so unspeakable that only the most devoid of humanity could bear to whisper its name.

– 12 –

No Margin for Error

Macua, Hong Kong

THE PRIVATE jet's landing gear kissed the tarmac at Hong Kong airport, its engines a fading whine in the humid night. Macau's neon kaleidoscope loomed across the Pearl River Delta, a city of glittering facades and hidden motives. Kang Hyuk, his angular face unreadable behind his mask of determination, clutched the slim case containing the RFCU, his enforcers forming a tight phalanx as they disembarked. Lin Sijue, cloaked in Dr. Maya Chan's emerald dress, followed, walking briskly to keep up, her heels clicking on the concrete. The drive to the casino hotel was a blur of sodium-lit highways, just the occasional murmur from Kang to the driver to seek an alternate lane through the heavy traffic to speed up their arrival.

The casino staff ushered them in with flattery as usual, and they quickly headed for Kang's suite. On the way, Lin's burner phone vibrated. She pulled it out of her cross-body and checked it making sure to keep the screen from Kang's eyes. It was a message from Peter. Her chest constricted. For a tense moment, she struggled with herself, not knowing what to do. But Kang forced her hand.

"Is something the matter?" he asked, shifting his full attention to her for the first time since leaving the Black Hand compound.

Lin reflexively fell back on to what she felt most comfortable with. "It's my boss. He wants me to join a conference call."

"I see," Kang said knowingly, as if he had already predicted this event.

"I had better take this," Lin said, looking for an out.

"I suppose you had better take it then," Kang said smoothly.

"Yes, will you excuse me?"

Kang gestured for one of his men to shadow her.

Lin peeled away and went to the front desk where she requested a conference room.

A service attendant took her across the foyer to the elevators. After a short ride to the 4th floor, he directed her down a hallway to a glassed room.

Lin thanked him. Kang's henchman waited outside.

"Codeword," Lin began.

"Monte Cristo," Peter replied.

"Yours?"

"Temple Storm."

"I'm sorry," was the first thing Peter said.

"No, I'm sorry," Lin said. She meant it. But she was grateful for Peter's rapprochement.

"I'm here."

"You're here?"

"I've checked into a room, 14th floor."

Lin looked at Kang's henchman. "I'm being watched," she said.

"Is there any way you could lose him?"

"I could, but it would risk my cover."

"Where are you?"

"I'm on the 4th floor, in a conference room."

"Head to the elevator shaft. Wait for the elevator to arrive. I'll take care of your problem, you head to the 13th floor, then take the stairs to the 14th."

When the elevator opened, Peter came out carrying a bucket of ice. He mock-tripped, emptying its contents onto the henchman. He made a scene, profusely apologizing, blocking the henchman from following Lin. Meanwhile, Lin boarded the elevator and headed to the 13th floor.

As soon as Lin saw Peter she embraced him, burying her nose in his hair. He clasped her in his strong arms. She felt the warmth of his body and let her muscles relax.

When they released, he said, "Come on." He took her to his room, closed the door and they kissed passionately, their lips searching, hungry.

Peter stroked her face, and whispered sorry again.

Lin shook her head and said, "No. I'm sorry."

He studied her. She seemed to be distraught.

"Crane was right," she said, unwillingly. "Kang's planning an attack."

Peter's face hardened. "Where?"

"I haven't been able to find out. Crane seems to think it will be on foreign soil."

"What sort of attack?"

"Not sure. But Kang's acquired a device that controls missiles."

"What kind of missiles?"

"Solid-rocket, various types of solid rockets."

Peter momentarily fell into thought. "It's unlikely he'd get access to a large one, so we have to assume he'll need to be close to his target in order to achieve a strike."

"I suppose so."

"As much as I hate to say this, you need to stay close to

Kang and find out."

Lin nodded. But her expression turned to one of anguish.

"What is it?"

"I hear you, but ... I don't want to do this anymore."

Peter reached for her hand, to sooth her. "I understand."

Lin pulled away. "No you don't understand. I had to kill you again!"

"Woah." He shifted uncomfortably. "You're saying another me? Again?"

"Yes! In Dandong."

"Dandong? What was I doing in Dandong?"

"You had a team. You came through the windows, engaged Kang's men in a firefight. Kang seemed to be prepared and repelled the attack. You fled to the rooftop where you struggled with one of his men. I got there just as you went over the edge. I managed to get hold of your wrist, but then ..."

"Then what?"

"You said the wrong code word again."

"Rusty's bark?"

"Yes."

"So you ..." He trailed off, unwilling to say what he knew to be true.

"I let you fall."

Peter sagged. Shook his head. "Crane sidelined me so he could use me."

"Both of us."

Peter jumped up and started pacing back and forth angrily. "He's got us in a bind, you realize that?"

"I know. It's crazy."

"It's got to stop."

Lin agreed. But then she reflected and said, "Yes, but there's a paradox."

Peter stopped pacing and stared at her.

"As inhumane as Crane's strategy is, it has allowed me to gain Kang's trust."

It wasn't what he wanted to hear. He looked away.

"If we don't stop him, innocent people will die," Lin said.

"I know," Peter said mechanically.

"But without a plan ..."

Peter said, "The RFCU. What about that?"

"Not a chance. He guards it like a dog with a bone."

"Then we need another diversion."

"Ok ..."

"I can trigger a fire alarm—this place will go crazy. Kang will grab the device and take it with him. That's when I jump him."

Lin's eyes narrowed, unconvinced. "With all his men around him?"

"It's either that or Kang gets away. Do you have a better idea?"

Lin took a while before answering. "No."

When it came time, Lin returned to the casino floor, the chandeliers' clatter of chips and laughter jarring after the dim room. Kang held court at the baccarat tables, his wolfish face impassive as he raked in winnings, a king in his gilded arena. She slipped into Maya Chan's mask, her smile a honed facade, her heart racing with their plan.

The alarm's shriek tore through the casino's carefully orchestrated ambiance like a chainsaw through bamboo. Emergency strobes began flashing, their harsh light splintering the crowd's movements into a stroboscopic nightmare of panic and confusion. Patrons surged toward the exits in waves of barely controlled hysteria, their shouts creating a chaotic symphony of fear and indignation.

Dealers abandoned their tables with practiced efficiency, leaving behind scattered chips like the remnants of broken promises. Security personnel materialized from hidden positions, their radios crackling with rapid-fire communications in Cantonese and English and what sounded like Russian.

Lin moved against the tide of fleeing gamblers, her trained eyes catching Kim's stumbling form as he was herded toward an exit by one of Kang's enforcers. She intercepted them at the mouth of a service stairwell, the alarm's wail softening to a more manageable level in the enclosed space.

"I've got him," she told the enforcer with Maya Chan's

authoritative snap. "I'll keep him in a tight leash."

The enforcer hesitated for a moment—long enough for Lin to wonder if her cover was blown—then nodded and melted back into the crowd, probably eager to return to his primary responsibility of protecting the RFCU.

Kim's breath reeked of whiskey and fear, but his eyes held a clarity that suggested the alcohol had been more performance than consumption. "What kind of missile are they planning on firing?" she demanded, her voice barely audible above the alarm. "Conventional? Nuclear?"

Kim shook his head. "No."

"What do you mean no. What else could it be?"

"I'm not sure. But I heard his sister is delivering the warhead."

Lin scratched her head. That didn't sound good. "His sister," she intoned vaguely.

"Yes, so if I had to guess, I'd say it's something biological."

Lin felt her chest tighten as if someone had wrapped steel cables around her ribs. The dread that had been her constant companion since Bangkok coiled tighter, becoming something that threatened to strangle her from the inside. A biological weapon—not just a bomb or a conventional terror attack, but something that could spread like wildfire through a population, turning human biology against itself.

"San Francisco, right?" Lin asked.

Kim nodded in the affirmative.

"How many people are we talking about?"

Kim's face cracked into a half terrifying, half crazy facade. "Millions. Tens of millions. Maybe more, depending on how far it spreads before anyone realizes what's happening."

The words no one wanted to hear. This wasn't terrorism—it was genocide with a technological twist, the kind of weapon that could reshape the global balance of power by simply eliminating inconvenient populations.

Boots thudded on the stairs above them, heavy and relentless. Two of Kang's enforcers rounded the stairwell's bend, their assault rifles slung low but ready, eyes cutting through the dim emergency lighting like laser sights.

"Seong-Jin!" one shouted, his voice carrying the authority of someone accustomed to instant obedience.

Kim swayed dramatically, slumping against the concrete wall with theatrical despair. "Too much whiskey," he slurred, his performance worthy of a professional actor. "Everything spinning ..."

Lin looped an arm under his shoulders, Maya Chan's composure locking into place like armor plating. "He's drunk," she said, her tone carrying exactly the right mixture of annoyance and maternal concern. "I'll get him some fresh air."

The enforcers hesitated, their gazes probing for signs of

deception. For a moment that stretched like eternity, Lin wondered if they could see through the performance—if her accelerated heartbeat was visible in her throat, if her pupils were dilated with adrenaline, if the sweat gathering at her hairline would betray her.

But Maya Chan's reputation held. The enforcers gestured them forward with the casual authority of men who had never had their judgment questioned, and Lin helped Kim stumble toward the exit like a long-suffering companion dealing with a friend's embarrassing public intoxication.

Everyone gathered outside the casino in a swelling crowd as fire engines roared in, their sirens slicing the humid Macau night. Firemen rushed into the building, their silhouettes sharp against the neon blaze. Lin's eyes scanned the chaos, locking onto Kang, the slim metallic case of the RFCU clutched tightly in his grip, two bodyguards flanking him like stone sentinels. But then her gaze caught something else—two more of Kang's men, each cradling an identical metallic case, each shadowed by a pair of bodyguards in the teeming crowd. Her stomach twisted at the deception, the multiplicity of decoys. She spotted Peter, receding behind a ceiling pillar, his subtle head shake a signal: stealing the case was a no-go. The wheel of karma spun, and Lin dreaded her place in its reckoning.

– 13 –

The Authentic Lie

Mid-Air, South China Sea

THE PRIVATE jet's cabin was a pressurized cocoon of tension, the slipstream outside a relentless hiss as the lone stewardess rolled out a trolley of drinks. Beyond the oval windows, the South China Sea stretched into an abyss, its darkness echoing the dread coiling in Lin Sijue's stomach. As Dr. Maya Chan, she sat across from Kang Hyuk, she wondered why Kang had bundled her along with Kim into a van along with his henchmen without saying a word about where they were going. The Henchman that Peter had way-laid outside the elevator shaft was staring at her intently, his cold eyes full of revenge. Lin merely gave him a wan smile, pretending innocence. The Jet could conceivably take them to San Francisco, but when they went through customs, there was no mention of the destination by anyone.

Kim Seong-Jin slumped beside Kang, his face a hollow shell of coerced compliance, his eyes darting nervously to the RFCU case resting on the empty seat beside Kang like a sleeping predator. Two of Kang's bodyguards sat two rows back, their identical cases on their laps, their silent presence a coiled threat even in the cabin's deceptive calm.

The stewardess poured Beluga Gold Line vodka over ice without asking—evidently she knew Kang's preferences in advance. Kang raised his glass, the vodka catching the cabin's muted LED glow, his mood expansive. "We must not get ahead of ourselves," he said, his voice thick with self-satisfaction, "but for now, we can celebrate our first momentous step toward justice." His eyes glittered as they locked on Lin, daring her to betray a flicker of weakness.

Lin mirrored his toast, her glass steady despite the storm raging in her veins. Her smart-contacts tracked Kim's vital signs—heart rate spiking at 140 BPM, cortisol still surging like a warning flare. Kim raised his glass mechanically, as if strings pulled his limbs, his gaze fixed on the RFCU case as if it contained a venomous snake.

"We still face major hurdles before complete victory," Kang continued, his gaze settling on Lin, "but I think it's worth saying—both of you deserve praise for your contributions." His eyes narrowed slightly. "You, Maya, for thwarting that assault at Yalu Needle. You proved your loyalty again."

"My pleasure," Lin said, her voice calm, mirroring Kang's confidence.

"Although, there's one small matter that caught my attention." His tone turned syrupy with insinuation.

"Oh?"

"Did you intervene with that agent on the rooftop to finish him off—or help him?"

The question was not entirely unexpected, but nevertheless it took her by surprise. It took all of Lin's effort to maintain her composure, not expose herself with an unconscious movement, a subtle tell. "I tried to extract intel—who he was, how he knew about the exchange."

"And?"

"He chose to sacrifice himself rather than talk."

"How convenient."

Lin let the silence stretch, leaving Kang to stew in his own suspicion. Her smart-contacts registered a slight uptick in his pulse—a predator forced to retreat from uncertain prey.

Kang shifted his attention to Kim—easier quarry. "I'm also grateful to you for acquiring this controller," he said, patting the RFCU case beside him. "It must have taken considerable nerve." His tone carried a barbed edge, a clear jab at Kim's faltering courage during the Dandong exchange.

Kim's shoulders sagged, his fingers digging into the armrest. "Yes," he whispered, his voice barely audible, as if all the air had been sucked from his lungs.

Lin's tactical awareness sharpened with cold clarity: Kang's blind spot to her left, bodyguards two rows back, Kim a fragile variable in a deadly equation. She imagined lunging across the narrow table, her hands closing around Kang's throat, ending his smug reign. But the fantasy passed as quickly as she conjured it—too many variables, too much risk.

"Don't misunderstand me," Kang said, swirling his glass contemplatively. "We still face significant challenges. We're far from finished. But for now, we can savor this milestone."

To Lin's surprise, these words seemed to stir something in Kim, perhaps the thought of his two daughters and wife locked up somewhere, innocent victims in this deadly game. "You don't care that your so-called justice will kill millions?" he said, voice trembling with barely contained fury, each word a deliberate barb.

Kang flinched, caught off guard, his polished facade cracking. "Oh, is that it? You've suddenly grown a conscience? Realized that your family might not be such a fair trade after all?"

Kim squirmed. Kang's retort had hit their mark. "No one wants to lose a loved one," was all he manged to mumble.

"And you think I don't understand that?"

"No, I don't think you do."

"Are you calling me a monster?" His eyes gleamed, relishing the confrontation.

"Monsters are animals," Kim retorted. "They don't kill for pleasure."

"Ah, so I'm not a monster? Then what am I?"

"You're a psychopath. And a liar."

Kang smoothed the front of his shirt, his fingers lingering on the silk as if to steady himself. "Sometimes lies pave the way to greater truths," he said evenly. "That's the cost of justice."

"Justice?" Kim's voice rose despite himself. "What do innocent lives have to do with your justice? Playing God—"

"You forget we're fighting for survival," Kang interrupted, his tone sharpening down to a razor's edge. "The United States has strangled North Korea for decades. How many innocent lives has that cost?"

Kim looked away, stung by the truth within the lie. But he rallied, his voice low but resolute. "That may be true, but you ignore the 'why.' North Korea isn't free. It brainwashes its people from birth to worship corrupt leaders obsessed with egotistical power and strutting on the world stage. America has flaws, but it's a democracy. Do you even understand what that means?"

"You're asking me if I can comprehend what a democracy is?" Kang's voice was thick with recrimination.

Kim met his gaze, unwavering, his defiance a quiet fire that refused to be extinguished.

Kang laughed—a tight, self-conscious sound. "Of course I do. It's a system that lets the rich grow richer while the poor beg for scraps."

Kim shook his head. "That's not democracy. That's just human nature. True democracy, the core idea, is that it allows people the freedom to fail. Everything that democracy represents flows from that."

Kang's laugh deepened into something more guttural. "Yes! And so people fail, then whine about their failures! They blame the government instead of themselves. North Koreans see that as weakness. We value duty—what you contribute to your country, not what it owes you. You've clearly forgotten that lesson, which is why I've taken it upon myself to re-educate you."

"By holding my family hostage?"

"It's a means to an end. A lesson in loyalty and sacrifice."

"I don't need lessons from you. You're not my teacher—you're a terrorist."

Kang's mask shattered. In a flash, he lunged forward and clamped his hand around Kim's throat. It wasn't a gesture to incite fear. It was a genuine physical attack designed to extinguish the life from another soul. "My patience is exhausted, comrade. You'll do exactly as I say, and you'll keep your pathetic opinions to yourself."

Kim choked, his hands clawing uselessly at Kang's iron grip.

"That's enough!" Lin said. Her hand gripped onto Kang's forearm. Her body coiled with lethal purpose as she flashed a warning glance at Kang's bodyguards, who had risen, but immediately froze, recognizing the clarity of her intent.

Kang's eyes met hers—wild, feral, the civilized man replaced by something primitive and dangerous. But slowly, incrementally, his hands loosened. He released Kim and sat back, running his fingers through his hair in a self-conscious effort to restore his composure.

Kim folded over, gasping for air. Lin steadied him with a gentle touch, her presence calming as his breathing gradually evened.

Kang composure gradually returned as he directed his gaze out of the porthole window. Lin thought she could detect a hint of embarrassment in his features. The man who had moments early professed discipline and disdained weakness had just lost control. She made a mental note of this moment. Maybe it could prove useful later on.

The jet began its descent, a subtle shift in pressure signaling their approach to Hong Kong. Lin rose with practiced grace, her heels silent on the carpet. "A moment to freshen up," she said, her smile disarming Kang's lingering scrutiny. He nodded, already distracted by another pour of vodka and the stewardess's strategically revealing uniform.

In the jet's cramped lavatory, Lin hurriedly retrieved Kim's folded note from her undergarments. It contained a single sentence in Korean: *My two daughter's names are Hana and Min-Ji. My wife's name is Yoona. Kang is holding them hostage. Please save them if you can.* She remembered his silent plea for help during their first encounter. Passing a note represented escalated risk-taking. His direct criticism of Kang was a further dangerous step. Desperation was driving him, but desperation bred mistakes. And mistakes in their world meant death.

She gripped the basin and stared at her reflection— Maya Chan's face gazing back like a beautiful stranger. An impostor. While Kang, in his madness, was paradoxically authentic. *Yet if I don't stop him, millions will pay the price.* She splashed cold water on her face, the shock sharpening her focus, then blotted it dry with coarse paper toweling.

Returning to the cabin, she slipped back into Maya Chan's polished persona, her smile a flawless shield. Kang had recovered his equilibrium, droning on in Korean about the genius of the 'party' leaders, his voice a hypnotic dirge. Kim sat in silence, his face impassive and obedient. It was only his hands, which Lin noted were folded protectively in his lap, that revealed he had long ago switched off listening and was just biding his time.

The jet touched down in Hong Kong, tires screeching against tarmac. Kang's enforcers hustled them to a black

SUV, the RFCU case now cradled protectively in Kang's lap, its metallic surface gleaming with impersonal menace. Kim was pushed into the back seat, his demeanor increasingly passive-aggressive. Lin slid in beside him, catching his eye with a subtle glance that conveyed: *Play the game. Now is not the time to make your move.*

Macau's skyline loomed ahead, a jagged mosaic of ancient pagodas and gleaming towers, stitched together by a frenzy of electronic advertisements that banished the night sky, their restless glow a wound on the earth's dark flesh. "Tomorrow, Maya, we will progress to phase two of this mission," Kang said, not looking at her, but at the skyline. "Black Hand's vision begins in San Francisco. That is where ground truth will be revealed."

There it was again. But this time, a direct admission. The cat was fully out of the bag. In effect, he was telling her she was now his operative—a protégé of Black Hand.

She had to admit: it was smooth, as it was presumptive. Had she played her cards that well? Her decisive intervention when Kang had Kim by the throat seemed to have struck the right note—a trace of individuality. Not enough to raise suspicion, but just enough to give her persona depth. Three dimensions. Not a lackey. A thinker. The kind of asset Kang admired, because everyone else around him behaved like lapdogs. Although she knew there was a deeper motive, as always with these psychopaths. He had to prove that the man who had lost control in the cabin was a momentary aberration. He would ensure it would never happen again, and she would be his witness. In a strange way, she realized she had become his trophy. And in the days ahead, he would likely show her off. She tucked that thought away—it would require another level of deception. Probably more tests. And maybe this was the real danger: that she wasn't pretending anymore. The line between Lin Sijue and Maya Chan was no longer blurring. It was dissolving.

– 14 –

The Voyage
South China Sea

THE ZEPPELIN *Celestial Phoenix* dominated Shek Kong Military Airfield's eastern edge, its silver envelope catching the first rays of sunlight breaking through Hong Kong's early morning mist. Two hundred meters of hydrogen-filled luxury strained against its mooring ropes like a thorough-bred stallion, the technology finally matured to withstand capricious air currents, lightning, and the dangers of static electricity. Lin had studied the technical specifications during her mission briefing: Platinum-class 'only' airship, maximum altitude fifteen thousand meters, range twelve thousand nautical miles, passenger capacity fifty-eight souls including crew of seven. What the specifications didn't capture was the opulent elegance of its dining room and cabins where Burmese teak met brushed titanium in soft rounded edges, and where molded plastics blended smoothly with designer fabrics to create a chic, understated aesthetic.

Lin couldn't help but feel a thrill as she boarded. This was her first voyage on a vessel like this, and she intended to savor it despite the dark moral cloud that hung over the mission's purpose. It wasn't that she could just compartmentalize it. She couldn't. But she wasn't going to let the responsibility of stopping a maniac from destroying the world ruin the exhilaration of the experience. She could do both. She had to.

The easiest solution would be to kill Kang now, throw him overboard in the middle of the South China Sea if necessary, although realistically, that was out of the question. He kept his four bodyguards close at all times, their movements displaying the particular economy of motion that marked Pyongyang's special forces training, creating an invisible forcefield around their boss. The lead enforcer, a bullish man whose face looked like it had been carved from granite with a dull chisel, took custody of the RFCU case with military efficiency, understated, methodical. Still, Lin noted the micro-tremor in his hands. Even Black Hand's most hardened operatives understood they were carrying something that could rewrite history.

Kang's suite occupied the forward section, its panoramic

windows offering an unobstructed view of whatever was about to unfold. He proudly showed it off to Lin before having her escorted to her own smaller cabin next to Kim's. Their quarters were situated opposite the dormitory cabins housing Kang's enforcers. Kim would be allowed to wander freely—there would be at least one enforcer shadowing him at all times of course—but he would essentially have free "run of the ship" until such time as he would be called up for "the special task he was brought along for." The way Kang said, and Lin's meager knowledge, she knew it had something to do with the activation codes that changed every 24 hours.

As Lin settled into her cabin, she noted the paper-thin walls. In the adjacent room, someone was having a heated conversation in Mandarin about payload deployment schedules. The acoustics meant every conversation became intelligence, every private moment a potential security breach.

Lin positioned herself by the starboard window as the *Celestial Phoenix* lifted off, Hong Kong's skyline contracting into a puzzle of glass and steel that befuddled the eye. Her reflection in the reinforced glass showed Maya Chan's face, but the eyes looking back belonged to someone she was losing the ability to recognize. How many layers of deception could a person sustain before the core self simply dissolved?

"Magnificent, isn't it?" Kang said, appearing beside her, close enough that she could smell his cologne—it was the first time she had sensed him wearing it. "Flying above the concerns of small people."

"Height provides perspective," Lin agreed, letting Maya's voice carry just enough ambiguity to keep him guessing. "Sometimes you see patterns that weren't visible from ground level."

"And sometimes you realize that the ground was never as solid as you thought." Kang shifted his weight from his shorter left leg to his right. It was a noticeable adjustment, and Lin wondered if he was slowly relaxing, letting his guard down now that she had proven her loyalty not once, but twice.

"Is there something you want to tell me?" Lin said, opting for directness. Take advantage while he was in a relaxed state of mind.

"I was thinking ..." He paused, looking out at the pewter-colored sea as it spread before them. "You never said a word either for me or against me when Kim had his little tantrum this morning." He turned fully toward her. "I'm sure you have an opinion. I'd like to hear it."

"Is this going to be another one of your tests?" Lin asked evenly.

"The time for testing is over. Feel free to express whatever opinion you think is right."

Lin slightly narrowed her eyes at him. So it was another test. "Kim said you were keeping his family hostage. Is that true?"

"It's merely a precaution so that he understands the stakes. After all, he stole a military-grade device and knows what it's for."

"You mean he might sabotage it?"

"It's certainly a possibility I haven't ruled out."

"In the plane I had the feeling he is already questioning the cost. His family for potentially millions. At some point something has to break."

"So long as he doesn't crack until it's done."

"And afterwards?"

"Afterwards ..." Kang broke into a confident smile. "We use the element of surprise to infiltrate deeper into the beast than ever before."

"I was talking about us."

Kang looked at Lin with mild surprise. "I assumed ..."

"You assumed?"

"That we would do it together."

"What exactly do you have in mind?" Lin inquired.

"I wouldn't be so arrogant as to assume you would be my mistress," Kang said cautiously. "I was thinking more along the lines of assigning you the position of advisor."

"Advisor," Lin said, tasting the word in her mouth. "But not equals."

Kang's face became serious. "Oh no, very much as equals."

"What about your sister?"

Kang's eyes momentarily flicked away. "She can look after herself."

"But she is also an advisor, is she not?"

"Are you jealous?"

Lin expected this remark. Kang's ego knew no bounds. She decided to play directly into it. "Yes, actually, I am."

Kang threw his head back and laughed. He was clearly enjoying himself. "Well, maybe you two will have to sort it out amongst yourselves."

Lin held her response. She merely smiled.

Kang appreciated that. He said, "Come on, I have an announcement to make."

When Kang entered the dining room, eighteen of the fifty available seats were occupied. Staff had been told to stay in their cabins and keep to themselves until food service was required. The airship, for all intents and purposes, was chartered by Chosun Precision Components, and what was to follow was for CPC 'employees' only. Kang ceremoniously popped the cork on a champagne bottle and had it passed around so everyone could get a sip in their glass.

"I want to raise a toast," he said, "to all the hard work that has brought us here." He scanned the dining room and settled his eyes on Kim, who was sitting close to the front where Kang held court. Kim's expression was sullen, and he raised his glass only high enough to avoid earning the ire of his brutal taskmaster. Lin watched all this with a sense of dark amusement, since she and Kim were effectively caged birds, and Kang could do as he pleased. They might as well play his macabre little game for what it was worth.

"In the last twenty-four hours, we have acquired a key component in our quest to rebalance the scales of justice, thanks to Kim Seong-Jin here." Kang clapped in praise of Kim, which spurred everyone else to follow suit. Kim gave a hesitant nod without a smile.

"In the next twenty-four hours, we will rendezvous with our great leader Bok Yeong, who will be bringing us the second component necessary to complete our mission, and we will marry them together here, aboard this vessel."

A dubious expression crossed Kim's face. Lin realized that this was the first time he had heard this news. But his reaction was quickly drowned out by cheers and clapping. The atmosphere had become festive, and Kang was happy to add fuel to the fire.

"Once the two components are integrated, we have only one more task ahead of us: to bring the entire 'package' to San Francisco. We have chosen this location as our target because it represents, more than any other city in the world, the heart of the AI revolution that we are fighting to defeat. Silicon Valley."

This was greeted by more cheers and clapping.

"And from this city, a pestilence will spread out and consume all of North America. There will be nothing they can do to stop it. They will try, but they will fail."

He reached into his pocket and pulled out a small ampule. Holding it up, he said, "This will keep our people safe. By the time they reverse-engineer it—if they can—it will be too late."

This time, rather than wild cheering and clapping, the collective attention was focused on the ampule holding an amber liquid, almost as if Kang were holding a sacred relic.

Lin would have loved nothing more than to snatch it from Kang's hand, but it would have been useless to try. Where could she go? Nowhere.

Lin's champagne glass trembled faintly in her hand, the crystal catching the dining room's candlelight as Kang tucked the ampule back into his pocket. The amber glow lingered in her mind like a vow of annihilation. His words—ten million souls in San Francisco, consumed by a pestilence—hung in the air like damp rot. The enforcers' cheers, fists pounding teak tables, drowned Kim's sullen silence, his untouched glass a rebellion too small to notice.

Lin's Maya Chan mask held, but her mind churned with questions: how would bio-weapon spread its deadly load?

A missile, arcing high to scatter death invisibly? Kang's secrecy—"there will be nothing they can do to stop it," he'd said—left her grasping in the dark. She needed Kim, his knowledge of the trigger, but the wiry enforcer with eyes like chipped flint who shadowed him everywhere would make any private conversation impossible.

As the *Celestial Phoenix* carved through dawn's mist, its silver envelope ghosting above the South China Sea's pewter waves, Lin found herself drawn to her cabin's starboard window. The reinforced glass was cool under her fingers, the prayer wheel in cross-body motionless, while the cosmos overhead relentless turned. Hong Kong's skyline had vanished hours ago, replaced by the Soko Islands' crumbling ruins—refugee shacks from a century past, their corrugated roofs sagging like broken promises.

Fishing junks bobbed far below, their red sails taut against the morning breeze, nets trailing like spectral webs in their wake. The stench of diesel exhaust wafted through the airship's ventilation system, a reminder of the world they'd left behind. A Chinese white dolphin surfaced near one of the junks, its pale fin a fleeting spark in the turquoise shallows, utterly oblivious to the death Lin carried in her mission.

Hours bled into the Philippine Sea, the airship's steady vibration a hypnotic drone against the occasional creak of Burmese teak expanding in the warming air. The Babuyan

Islands rose from the horizon like volcanic fangs cloaked in mist, their silence mocking Lin's growing urgency. Far below, rust-streaked freighters plowed lonely furrows through international waters, their deck cargo mere specks from ten thousand feet.

Near Palau, scattered fishing boats flickered like fireflies under dusk's purple veil. A humpback whale breached in the distance, its spout a smoke signal in the cobalt void, stirring something Lin couldn't name—a pang for life persisting, unaware of Black Hand's plague.

The central Pacific stretched endlessly, broken only by nameless atolls—coral rings glinting like shattered glass in the ocean's heart. Seabirds wheeled far below, frigate birds with crimson throat patches, their harsh cries sharp against the wind's low moan. Kim spent hours pacing the observation deck, his enforcer a constant shadow, his face etched with the absence of Hana, Min-Ji, and Yoona. Lin watched him through the panoramic windows, mapping her chances to reach him, feeling the RFCU's shadow grow heavier than the storm clouds gathering on the horizon.

Thirty-two hours out from Hong Kong, Wake Island materialized from the morning haze—a coral wishbone fringed by a lagoon that glowed like molten glass. The atoll sat alone in 3,700 miles of empty ocean, a desolate stage for what was to come. The *Celestial Phoenix*'s engines softened to a whisper as Captain Yuen brought them down to fifty meters, sea anchors plunging into the lagoon's calm lee where waves barely stirred the surface.

The airship hovered with mechanical precision, its silver bulk steady as water ballast jetted from its undercarriage in a hissing cascade. Lin pressed against the observation deck's windows, watching the sea below churn white with displaced air and water. The compensation was necessary—they were about to take on something heavy.

Bok Yeong's submarine breached like a surfacing leviathan, its sleek black hull slicing the lagoon's mirror-perfect surface. Foam churned as hatches parted with metallic clangs, and black-clad figures swarmed the deck with military efficiency. A hoist cable dropped from the airship's belly, its industrial winch groaning under strain as it lifted a wooden crate—six feet long, stenciled with Korean runes that Lin couldn't read, its contents a lethal mystery.

The missile, Lin knew with cold certainty. The delivery system that would rain spores over San Francisco.

The airship shuddered as more ballast hissed free, compensating for the crate's weight as it disappeared into the cargo hold with a dull, final thud. Bok stood on the submarine's conning tower, his angular frame taut with purpose, a pale scar bisecting his brow like a geological fault line. His eyes burned with the zealot's fire—a crusade against the West's perceived decadence made manifest in engineered death.

Kang watched from his suite's panoramic window, subtly adjusting his posture to accommodate his shorter leg as he pressed his palm against the glass. For once, Lin saw deference in his posture—a rare submission to someone even more fanatical than himself. Her fingers twitched with the urge to pry open that crate, to confirm the missile's design and capabilities. But the enforcers—six now, led by the granite-faced brute still clutching the RFCU case—guarded the cargo hold like attack dogs.

That evening, the dining room glowed with warm candlelight, its teak tables set for a feast that felt more like a last supper. Bok sat at the head table, his scar pale against his sallow skin, while Kang was relegated to his right—a subordinate's position that clearly rankled. Lin and Kim flanked them, eighteen enforcers filling the remaining seats, their various faces sharing a common lust for violence that had been bred into them since childhood.

The air was thick with the scents of a traditional North Korean banquet, crafted to honor the regime's elite: chilled *naengmyeon*, buckwheat noodles in tangy beef broth, served in silver bowls; pungent *kimchi*, its fermented spice sharp on the tongue; *sinseollo*, a steaming hot pot brimming with ginseng, abalone, and rare mushrooms, symbolizing the Leaders' eternal bounty; and delicate *songpyeon*, rice cakes stuffed with sesame paste, their crescent shapes a nod to Mount Paektu's moon. Premium rice wine, poured from lacquered flasks, gleamed in porcelain cups, the delicate clink of their toasts a fragile counterpoint to the engines' ever-present thrum.

"North Korea is the world's only true fortress," Bok began, his chopsticks poised like a conductor's baton. "Undefeated, pure, guided by the eternal wisdom of our Leaders. Their vision—Kim Il-sung, Kim Jong-il, Kim Jong-un—carves a path no enemy can break. The West crumbles under its own moral corruption while we stand as strong as tempered steel."

Kang nodded with appropriate reverence, his smile tight at the corners, while Kim stared at his plate as if it might reveal some escape route. His enforcer's eyes bored into him from across the table, a silent reminder of his family's precarious situation.

Lin sipped her wine, her Maya Chan mask serene, but her pulse raced with each word. This wasn't just fanaticism—it was the kind of absolute certainty that made genocide feel like duty.

"Our cities," Bok continued, his voice gaining fervor, "Pyongyang, Hamhung, Chongjin—built for unity, not the chaos of capitalist individualism. Our military, a million strong, guards our sacred soil. Mount Paektu, where our Leaders' revolutionary spirit was born, watches over us like a protective ancestor. The world will kneel before this truth, or it will burn in the fires of its own AI invincibility."

His words were a hymn to absolutism, each syllable a laser burning away nuance and humanity. The enforcers murmured their assent, chopsticks pausing in reverence as their leader painted genocide in the colors of righteousness.

Lin glanced at Kim, noting the tightness in his jaw, his thoughts likely on Hana, Min-Ji, and Yoona—trapped in that same "fortress" Bok glorified. She needed his truth, not Bok's propaganda, but the enforcer's constant gaze pinned them both to their roles.

After dinner, Bok led his inner circle to the smoking room—a teak-paneled sanctum heavy with the mingled scents of aged whiskey and premium cigars. Crystal bowls of mango sorbet sat untouched as Bok poured single malt with the precision of ritual, his movements economical and deliberate.

He reclined in a leather chair that had probably cost more than most people earned in a year, glass in hand, his scar catching the amber lamplight. When he spoke, his tone carried the casual authority of a man accustomed to absolute obedience.

"Kang," he said, the single word sharp enough to make the other man stiffen. "Dandong was a failure. The mission nearly collapsed into chaos. I want to know what happened."

Kang's face went rigid as he shifted uncomfortably on his shorter leg. "Our intelligence flagged a potential Russian Doll infiltration—I took the necessary steps, assigned extra men, and we successfully thwarted the attack. If I may say, Dr. Chan—" he gestured toward Lin, his smile forced and brittle—"she acted decisively and secured the RFCU, thereby ensuring our operational continuity."

Lin maintained her demure nod, but her mind raced with the irony. Dandong, where she'd played her role too well, sacrificing another Peter, had allowed Kang could walk away victoriously, while the vestige of her true self had been reduced to a funeral pyre.

Bok's pale eyes assessed her with the cold calculation of a predator evaluating prey. "A victory plucked from the jaws of defeat then," he said after a long moment, taking a measured sip of his whiskey. "But understand this clearly, Kang—there is no margin for further errors. The Leaders demand perfection, not excuses."

Having made this pronouncement, he rose from his chair, his angular frame casting a long shadow across the room's rich wood paneling. Without another glance at any of them, he exited with the fluid motion of a man secure in his own authority. The enforcers followed in his wake like a dark tide, leaving Kang slouched in his chair, already refilling his glass with hands that visibly shook, forcing him to gulp quickly to disguise the weakness.

The stress of maintaining face before Bok triggered something in Kang that Lin recognized from her psychological profiles—a binge pattern that manifested when his control was threatened. As the submarine sank back into the lagoon's depths and the *Celestial Phoenix* climbed toward its rendezvous with San Francisco, Kang retreated to his suite with a bottle of whiskey and his wounded pride.

Without gambling tables to distract him from Bok's rebuke, his consumption accelerated. Lin could hear him through the thin walls—laughter slurring into curses, furniture scraping across deck plates, the clink of glass against glass growing more frequent and less steady.

The enforcers, lulled by their leader's self-imposed isolation, relaxed their constant vigilance. Kim, sensing an opportunity, slunk away, finding a narrow maintenance corridor where he could nurse his grievances alone.

Lin found him sitting with his back against a bulkhead, head between his knees.

The space was cramped and thick with the smell of machine oil and heated metal, but it offered something precious—a few minutes away from constant surveillance.

"Seong-Jin," she whispered, her voice barely audible over the airship's ambient noise. "We need to talk."

Kin looked up. His eyes looked sunken in the dimly lit corridor. "Go away!" he said, and buried his head between his knees again.

"This is not time to feel sorry for yourself," Lin berated him. "You heard Bok's speech. I need you to tell me what we are dealing with here."

Kim looked up again. "You want to know what we are dealing with?" he asked sarcastically.

"Yes," Lin replied seriously.

"Bok belongs to a generation of megalomaniacs who see their fellow humans as nothing more than tools to realize their ideological fantasies. Whether those fantasies have any relationship to reality is irrelevant to them."

"I don't doubt that. But what is this 'pestilence' that Kang spoke of? I know you said it would be a biological weapon. But what type? If we can forewarn—"

Kim brutally cut her off. "You don't understand. They engineered this weapon using AI. You can bet on that. So whatever type of pestilence it is, you can be sure that there is no possibility of stopping it without access to its actual design parameters. And the only way to get that is you need to directly infiltrate the mainframe at Black Hand's facility in Liaoning. And I don't see that happening."

"Wait a minute. Did you say the design parameters are stored in the Liaoning mainframe?"

"Yes. That's the assumption."

"I planted a nano interceptor in their communications hub."

Kim laughed. "The only reason you were able to do that was because they let you. They want you to think you succeeded."

Lin flushed with disappointment, and something else, fear.

"Don't tell me ..." Kim said.

"It was unavoidable."

Kim pulled an anguished face, ran his hands through his hair.

"Then ... the only chance we have is for you to somehow delay giving him the access code, until ..."

"Until what?"

"Until we can stop him somehow."

Kim his head between his knees again. "What have I done?"

Lin tried to reassure him. "I would have done the same if it was my family. You did nothing wrong."

Kim looked up at her. "You think so?" His eyes were deploring, but he knew the truth.

Lin didn't have the heart to tell him.

Footsteps echoed from the main corridor. Lin signaled silence with a subtle gesture, both of them freezing as the sound passed. The airship's conduits pulsed around them like mechanical arteries, carrying power and information through the vessel's metallic nervous system.

When the danger passed, Lin placed her hand briefly on Kim's shoulder, her voice low and resolute. "I swear, I'll help your family get out of North Korea—if you play your part."

Kim's eyes shone bright with hope. "You will?"

"If it's the last thing I do."

– 15 –

Betrayal
San Francisco, United States

THE Pacific fog rolled in like a living thing, swallowing the California coast in its gray embrace. From the *Celestial Phoenix*'s observation deck, Lin could barely make out the water's surface fifty meters below—the world had become a study in porcelain and shadow, the airship suspended in a void between sea and sky. The fog muffled sound, creating an eerie cocoon around the vessel as it drifted toward the rendezvous point.

Captain Yuen's voice crackled over the intercom, steady despite the challenging conditions: "Visibility down to eighty meters and falling. Sea anchors ready for deployment on my mark."

Lin pressed against the dining room's starboard window,

the reinforced glass cool beneath her palm. Through the murk, she caught glimpses of the Pacific's pewter surface, glassy with the absence of any wind. Somewhere in that gray maze, Kang's luxury motor cruiser waited to take possession of death itself.

The airship's engines shifted to a whisper as water ballast hissed from the undercarriage in preparation. They would need to compensate for the wooden crate's weight once it was transferred—six feet of engineered destruction that would soon be unleashed on ten million unsuspecting souls.

"Contact established," came the radio operator's voice. "Motor vessel *Jade Emperor* bearing two-seven-zero, range four hundred meters."

Through the fog's shifting curtains, Lin caught her first glimpse of Kang's cruiser—a sleek cutter of white fiberglass and chrome, its twin diesel engines purring with barely contained power. Forty meters of luxury that would serve as the missile's final transport vehicle.

The sea anchors plunged with muffled splashes, their chains rattling as the *Celestial Phoenix* settled into position. A hoist cable dropped from the cargo bay, swaying like a mechanical pendulum in the still air. Lin watched the operation unfold with clinical detachment, memorizing every detail for the intelligence report she might never file.

Kang emerged from his suite, his compensated gait held

firmly in check. His earlier drunken stupor had been replaced by focused intensity—the gambling addict's high when the final bet was placed. Behind him, Kim walked with the hollow resignation of a man watching his soul being bartered away piece by piece.

"Dr. Chan," Kang said, approaching Lin with his wolfish face that she'd learned to read like weather patterns. "Would you care to observe the transfer from closer quarters? This is history in the making."

Lin nodded with Maya's practiced enthusiasm. "I wouldn't miss it for anything in the world."

The first transfer began with mechanical precision. Kang descended first, riding the hoist platform like a conquering general, his four bodyguards flanking him in perfect formation. Their movements displayed the particular economy of trained killers—no wasted motion, every gesture calculated for maximum efficiency.

Kim followed on the second descent, his face pale against the fog's gray backdrop. Lin could see the war playing out behind his eyes—love for his family wrestling with knowledge of what his compliance would unleash. The enforcer assigned to shadow him never let the distance between them exceed arm's reach.

The wooden crate came last, emerging slowly from cargo bay doors beneath the airship, swaying gently on its cable as it descended through the fog. Lin held her breath as it reached the cruiser's deck, its piano-size bulk and weight straining against its straps. Kang's men grabbed on to it and guided it down into a large hatch, its doors laid open like a mouth ready to devour whatever fed it. The granite-faced enforcer who'd guarded it so jealously now supervised its detachment from the hoist cable, while Kang craned his neck this way and that, following it, calling out "left, right, a little more to the left ..." like a foreman on a job site. The hoist went slack and spooled back into the airship, signifying that its deadly cargo was finally secured.

Lin was so focused on the operation that she almost missed the tanker's horn—three long blasts that cut through the fog like an air raid siren. The sound came from their starboard side, close enough to make the *Celestial Phoenix*'s hull vibrate with sympathetic resonance.

"Emergency stations!" Captain Yuen's voice cracked over the intercom. "Tanker bearing zero-nine-zero, range two hundred meters and closing fast!"

Through the fog's gray veil, Lin glimpsed the behemoth's bulk—a supertanker the size of a small city, its rust-streaked hull cutting through the water with inexorable momentum. Men scrambled across its forecastle deck, shouting at the motor cruiser to get out of the way.

Kang's men, seeing the monster bearing down on them, jumped into action like startled monkeys. They slammed the cargo hold hatches down and cast off their temporary lines. The engines roared to life, and the *Jade Emperor* leaped forward like a startled fish.

The tanker's horn blared again, closer now. Lin could see the collision lights flashing through the fog, red and white strobes that painted the mist in hellish colors. The super-tanker's captain was doing everything possible to avoid disaster, but physics had its own merciless logic.

Kang's cruiser carved a tight turn to port, its twin propellers churning the water to white foam. They sped away from the tanker's prow with seconds to spare. Lin watched from the airship's dining room as the white hull vanished into the fog, carrying death toward San Francisco's unsuspecting millions.

The tanker noiselessly slipped beneath the *Celestial Phoenix*, its superstructure passing so close that Lin could see individual rivets in the hull plating. Men on the forecastle were scanning frantically for signs of collision, their faces taut with the particular terror that came from being helpless passengers on a ship they couldn't control.

But the physics worked in their favor. The airship's sea anchors held position while the tanker's momentum carried it safely past, its wake rocking the *Celestial Phoenix* like a cradle. Within minutes, both vessels had vanished into the fog's gray embrace, leaving only the lingering scent of diesel exhaust and the memory of disaster barely averted.

"All stations secure," Captain Yuen announced, his voice steady once more. "Resume normal operations. Prepare for final approach to San Francisco Airfield."

Lin remained at the window as the fog began to thin, revealing glimpses of the California coast. The Golden Gate Bridge's towers emerged from the mist like ancient monuments, their International Orange paint a splash of color against the gray morning. Below, the city sprawled in all its chaotic glory—ten million souls going about their daily lives, utterly unaware that death had just taken up residence in their midst.

The *Celestial Phoenix* touched down at San Francisco Airfield with barely a tremor, its silver envelope settling onto the tarmac like a sleeping giant. Ground crews swarmed around the mooring points, their movements efficient despite the lingering fog that reduced visibility to mere meters.

Lin gathered her few belongings, her mind already racing ahead to the next phase of the mission. She needed to contact Crane, warn him about the missile now hidden somewhere in the city's labyrinthine infrastructure. The trick was to get away from Kang's handlers.

The customs hall at San Francisco Airfield buzzed with the controlled chaos of international arrivals. Passengers from the *Celestial Phoenix* queued at immigration desks, their documents scrutinized by uniformed officers whose bored efficiency masked the routine nature of their work. The fog had followed them inside, seeming to cling to windows and seep through ventilation systems.

Lin presented her Maya Chan passport with practiced confidence, the documents pristine forgeries that had passed inspection at a dozen border crossings. The customs officer—a seemingly docile man whose name tag read "Tanaka"—scanned the pages with mechanical precision.

"Purpose of visit?" he asked without looking up.

"Business," Lin replied, letting Maya's slight accent color the word. "Biochemical consulting."

Tanaka nodded, but instead of stamping the passport, he made a subtle gesture toward a side corridor. "Ma'am, if you could step this way for a moment? We need to verify some additional documentation."

Lin's instincts screamed danger, but Maya Chan had no reason to refuse. She followed Tanaka toward a door marked "Secondary Screening," aware of Kang's enforcers watching from the main line. The granite-faced brute who'd guarded the RFCU case caught her eye, his expression questioning.

"Just routine," she called out with Maya's bright smile. "You know how thorough American customs can be."

The enforcer nodded grudgingly, but she could see suspicion building behind his scarred features. Time was their enemy now—every minute that passed brought them closer to the missile's launch window.

Inside the screening room, Tanaka closed the door with deliberate care. The space was sterile and windowless, designed to intimidate nervous travelers into compliance. But Lin wasn't nervous—she was calculating distances, escape routes, the location of every potential weapon.

"Dr. Chan," a familiar voice said from the shadows. "Or should I say, Lin?"

A figure stepped from behind a privacy screen—tall, angular, wearing the uniform of a senior customs official. But Lin recognized the voice, the predatory grace of movement. Agent Martinez from Russian Doll, his cover so perfect that even his credentials would pass official scrutiny.

"There's been a change of plans," Martinez said, producing a small device that looked like a standard medical scanner. "Hold still."

The sedative was administered through what appeared to be a routine biometric check—a brief pressure against her wrist that delivered fast-acting ketamine through her skin. Lin felt the familiar blur creeping across her vision, her muscles loosening against her will.

"Her papers require additional verification," Tanaka was saying to someone outside the door, his voice growing distant. "Immigration hold. Could be several hours."

Through the fog of sedation, Lin heard Kang's enforcer demanding answers, his voice sharp with suspicion. But Tanaka's response was bureaucratically perfect: "Look, pal, I don't make the rules. Homeland Security flagged her documentation. You want to wait around for the paperwork, be my guest. Otherwise, I suggest you move along before I start asking questions about your own status."

The enforcer's curses were muffled by the closing door, but Lin caught the gist. Time was slipping away, and Kang's operation couldn't afford delays. They would have to proceed without Maya Chan, at least temporarily.

"Smart move," Martinez said, catching Lin as she slumped forward. "No violence, no suspicious circumstances. Just bureaucratic red tape doing what it does best."

The last thing Lin saw before darkness claimed her was Tanaka opening another door, one that led not to immigration processing but to a loading dock where a nondescript van waited in the fog. Russian Doll had found her, and they'd done it with the quiet efficiency that made them so dangerous.

– 16 –

Mind in Perpetuum
San Francisco, United States

CONSCIOUSNESS returned in sluggish waves, each one carrying a tide of nausea. Lin was strapped to a gurney in a mobile laboratory parked near an airfield tarmac in San Jose, its sterile steel surfaces and thrumming electronics a stark contrast to the fog outside. IV lines snaked from her arms to bags of clear fluid overhead. The room rocked gently, suggesting they were aboard a disguised vehicle.

She strained against the restraints. "Why am I tied down? What is this?"

Crane stepped into view, his craggy face tired from the early morning flight. "Precaution, Lin. Your mission is over. We're archiving your operational profile and sending in EVE-7 to replace you."

Lin's blood curdled. "So it's true. You've cloned us."

"Yes," Crane admitted, his voice devoid of remorse. "But it's for your own good. We intercepted intel from Bok's submarine. Kang no longer trusts you. He was going to kill you the moment you arrived in San Francisco. We stepped in to save your life."

"But in exchange, you're sending in my clone to die," Lin said, straining against the straps with renewed fury.

"We've been through this before, Agent Sijue," Crane replied flatly. "You know it's the right choice."

"Let me out of here!" Lin demanded, her voice raw.

"Not until Quinn has finished with you," Crane said, nodding to Dr. Avery Quinn, who stood ready by a neural mapping console. "First, we need a full-spectrum memory capture. To imprint your recent experiences onto EVE-7's behavioral matrix. Seamless integration is key."

Lin struggled violently, but the restraints held firm. "You can't do this!"

Dr. Quinn adjusted a headset above Lin's brow, its sensors glowing faintly. "Initiating targeted memory extraction. Prioritizing hippocampal engrams from the last operational cycle—trauma bonds, tactical adaptations, key interpersonal data. The clone's implant is an empty vessel without this foundational dataset."

Lin continued to struggle.

"Don't fight it, Lin. It will do you no good," Raskova said, in an even, motherly tone. "We'll sedate you again when the process is finished." The machine began crunching its stacked algorithms, sifting through her neural noise to identify and copy the most strategically valuable memories.

Satisfied that Lin was stable, Raskova went over to EVE-7, strapped to an identical gurney—Lin's perfect physical duplicate, eyes closed, face serene under Raskova's ministrations. Wires connected the clone to banks of monitors displaying cascading genetic and neural data.

Crane watched Quinn's progress. As Lin's struggles subsided into mumbled delirium, Raskova turned to him, her voice clinical.

"I think we have to be honest," Raskova said. "The two Harrington clones were failures not because of integration, but because of context. They were perfectly adequate against Black Hand's men, but failures against our own."

"You're saying that our agents know too much about each other for them to fool each other."

"Yes."

Next to them, Lin mumbled, "Peter! Peter! Don't trust them!"

Crane hushed her. "It's ok, Agent Sijue. Consider yourself lucky. The Lazarus archive will preserve a perfect record of your experiences. I'm saving you from yourself."

"Lazarus ..." Lin said, murmuring the word.

"Yes," Crane said. "Your memories will become part of his grand design."

"Lazarus ..." Lin repeated.

"You are providing the raw material for his children," Crane said, proudly. "We're nearly there. If everything goes according to plan, this will be the last time we have to ever send in a real person."

"Peter! Will he ... die?"

"The operational parameters assure us the odds of success are worth the risk."

"Please don't let him die!"

"If he dies," Crane said, calmly, "then I will give you his clone."

"But he won't be real!"

"Oh, he'll be real enough... He will have the same memories, the same conditioning. He will be a perfect facsimile. Just like EVE-7."

Lin closed her eyes, drained.

Crane watched her settle into a semi-conscious state, her breathing gradually slowing, her muscles loosening against the straps.

"She'll be all right," Raskova said.

Crane nodded, thanked Raskova and Quinn, and walked out into the morning light.

Outside, the heavy fog swirled around the tarmac lights. The mobile laboratory, disguised as a maintenance truck, was parked near a hangar. Crane spotted Justine Fairweather waiting beside a sleek, unmarked sedan, bundled in a warm coat. As he approached her, her sharp eyes tracked a newly arrived black sedan as it pulled up next to theirs. Crane followed her gaze, recognized Peter in the passenger seat, and altered his path. He went to the black sedan and knocked on the window.

Peter lowered the window.

"There's a team waiting for you at the maintenance sheds. I want you to debrief them."

"The mission?"

"You'll be intercepting Kang and his men at a warehouse in Silicon Valley."

"What about Lin?"

"I've withdrawn her from the mission."

Peter raised his eyebrows. "Why?"

"Her cover's blown. Sending her in would be suicide."

Peter nodded.

Crane said, "If you can, I want you to extract a hostage that Kang is holding. His name is Kim Seong-Jin. But only after you stop him from launching his rocket at us."

"Rocket?"

"If that rocket flies, who knows how many will die. You need to stop it. Whatever it takes."

"Understood."

Crane slapped the roof of the vehicle. "I'm counting on you, Harrington. Don't fuck this one up."

Peter raised his window and signaled the driver to move out.

Crane watched the vehicle drive toward the maintenance sheds, then signaled Fairweather to get in.

Sliding into the rear seat beside her, Crane said, "We're on the clock now."

Justine nodded. "What did you tell him?"

Crane fastened his seatbelt, his gaze fixed ahead through the fogged windshield. "I told him that I pulled Agent Sijue out and that he'll be taking her place."

"I see," Fairweather said softly. Then with more bite, "And what happens if he runs into EVE-7 while he's there?"

"He'll arrive later. He first has to debrief his men. Hopefully, EVE-7 will have talked Kang out of his foolish scheme by then and I'll be able to stand Peter down."

"You think so?"

"No, but it's the best opening gambit I've got. You think you've got a better one?"

"How about just launch a direct strike on the warehouse?"

"And risk dispersing the biological material, not to mention kill Kang's hostage?"

"Weren't you the one that said, 'Sometimes you have to burn something down to let something new grow.'" She gazed at him coolly with her hazelnut eyes.

Crane nodded sagely. "True. But in this case, we only want to do that as a last resort. I think you agree."

Fairweather nodded and waved for the driver to take them to the waiting chopper at the other end of the tarmac.

Meanwhile, the neural mapper continued its relentless work, and Lin felt her mind begin to fragment—not into silence, but into discrete, catalogued memories. Her recent experiences were unspooled like film through a projector, each frame lit with pain, love, and betrayal, tagged and copied. She saw the muzzle flash as she executed the first Peter clone in Kang's compound, his blood warm on her hands. The pressure of Kang's grip returned—the way he pinned her in his private room, the stench of soju on his breath, the bruises she never spoke of. She saw the second Peter clone's terrified eyes as she let go of his hand, watching him vanish through the fog beneath the Yalu Needle. And then, a flicker of peace: her grandmother's ghost in the storm-lit temple, mouth moving in a language older than revolution. All of it recorded, archived, stripped from her like skin from bone to be used as a script for her double.

She floated above herself, detached, and for the first time, she thought she had caught a glimpse of what it might be like to be unmade. It wasn't death, but something more insidious: being reduced to a data set. It didn't frighten her. Not because it should, but because it wasn't something she could fully comprehend. True death, she realized, was the end of consciousness. But here, the most intimate parts of her mind were being copied, to be woven into another body that looked identical to her, but was just a puppet running on her stolen memories. Would that puppet continue on? Is that what Lazarus wanted? Or did he want more?

– 17 –

Terminal Countdown
San Francisco, United States

THE WAREHOUSE was a cavern of forgotten industry, its vastness swallowed by shadows that clung to corrugated steel walls. High above, several of the grime-caked skylight panels had been removed, leaving a large opening that exposed the dull gray bowl of the sky. The missing panels allowed weak, dusty beams of afternoon light to slant into the cavernous space, illuminating floating motes of rust and decay. A mobile launch rail was positioned directly beneath the hole, and was loaded with a sleek missle. The light that poured in reflected off its shiny white paintwork giving it the appearence of a showroom piece, belying its sinister purpose. The air was thick with the smells of cold concrete and diesel. Across the floor, a web of thick, temporary power cables presented a maze of trip hazards, their presence underscored by the sharp buzz of a corded drill and the snapped orders of Kang Hyuk as he directed his men through the final stages of the setup.

At the center of this cavernous space, bathed in the clinical white glow of portable halogen lamps, stood the reason for it all. The missile was not some towering ICBM, but a compact, sinister-looking cylinder, seven feet long, painted a dull, non-reflective black. It rested on a mobile launch rail, its nose cone housing the unthinkable.

Kang Hyuk stood before it, a high priest at a profane altar. His posture was rigid, the usual slight adjustment for his shorter leg held in perfect check by sheer will. "Now, Seong-Jin," he said, his voice rising above the activity around them, "it's time for you to show me your loyalty to our cause."

Kim Seong-Jin, his hands trembling so violently he could barely hold the fiber-optic cable, knelt before the RFCU—the Remote Firing Control Unit—as he prepared to connect it to the data socket of the launch system. His face was a mask of sweat and crazed concentration. "The synchronization protocol ... it's delicate. A single misaligned pin—"

"Get it wrong, and it will be the last mistake you ever make," Kang finished, his tone that of a harsh school master. He didn't need to brandish a weapon; the threat was a physical presence in the room. His four enforcers, stationed at the warehouse's cardinal points, were testament to that.

Near the missile's tip, Kang's sister, Soo-Min, worked with an unnerving, robotic grace. Dressed in a black bio-hazard suit, its hood thrown back to reveal a face as sharp and cold as her brother's, she carefully loaded the payload canister—a stainless steel cylinder no larger than a ther-mos—into the access port. It clicked into place with a sound that signaled the grim finality to the process.

"The spores are active and stable," Soo-Min reported, her voice devoid of inflection. "The dispersal mechanism is armed."

A triumphant, wolfish smile spread across Kang's face. "Excellent." He turned to Kim. "Are you ready to elevate?"

Kim had completed the yoking between the RFCU and the launch system. "Yes," he said feebly.

With a low hydraulic whine, the launch rail began to tilt, raising the missile to a seventy-five-degree angle, aiming it at the hole at the center of the roof panels that had been removed. The target was not a coordinate on a map, but the demographic epicenter of Silicon Valley.

"Now, the code," Kang said, as the sound of activity around them dropped to a hush. He drew a pistol from his shoulder holster, not with haste, but with a terrible, delib-erate finality. He aimed it at Kim almost casually, as if it was a mere formality. "The twelve-digit sequence. Input it."

Kim stared at the keypad, his finger hovering. He was a coward, yes. He didn't want to die. But the image of his daughters, Hana and Min-Ji, and his wife, Yoona, flashed before his eyes. Was trading their lives for millions justified? Was there any justification?

"Think of your family, Seong-Jin," Kang said, sensing his hesitation. "Input the code, and you will have the antidote. You will be a hero of the Republic, and your family will want for nothing. Refuse ..." He let the silence hang, more potent than any shout.

Kim wiped the sweat from his eyes—which was pouring profusely now—with the back of his sleeve. His finger, shaking uncontrollably, moved toward the keypad.

Almost at the same time, outside, Peter Harrington and his team arrived and took up stealthy positions at distance from the warehouse. Peter raised his high-powered binoculars and searched for a window or an opening that allowed him to see what was going on inside. He noted four men stationed at each corner, scanning for any suspicious activity. Running his eye along the building, he found a window that gave him a direct view of his target.

"Echo Team in position," he whispered into his throat mic. "One launcher, one missile. Kang, four tangos, one female technician, and the asset, Kim. The package is vertical." His SEAL training took over, compartmentalizing the horror into manageable data points.

A sudden movement at the warehouse's main entrance caught his eye. A side door opened, and a figure stepped into the pool of light.

It was Lin.

Peter's couldn't believe his eyes. She was here! How? Crane had told him she had been taken out of the loop.

She walked directly toward Kang, her stride confident, but her face was a complex map of emotions that gave Peter a moment's pause.

"Kang," she said, her voice clear, breaking the hushed silence.

Kang turned. His expression shifted from impatience to something else—a flicker of confusion, a momentary delay as if searching a corrupted file. The glitch passed, replaced by amused curiosity. "Maya. The American bureaucracy released you. I trust the delay wasn't too ... inconvenient?"

"Stop this, Kang," Lin said, ignoring his taunt. She stopped a dozen feet from him, her gaze fixed on his. "Look at what you're about to do. This isn't justice. It's a monstrosity."

Kang chuckled, a low, condescending sound. "Monstrosity is a subjective term, Doctor. This is pest control. We are excising a cancer. The code, Kim!"

"Don't!" Lin commanded, her voice ringing with an authority that made Kim freeze. Her hand moved to the small of her back and came up holding a compact semi-automatic pistol. She aimed it directly at Kang's chest. "I will shoot you. Order him to stand down."

The atmosphere crystallized. The enforcers shifted, their weapons coming up. Kang's own pistol was still in his hand, but he didn't raise it. He just stared at her, that strange, half-confused look in his eyes again.

"Do it!" He shouted at Kim, pressing his pistol barrel against Kim's head.

Kim mumbled something and relented. His hand turned a key. There was a beeping sound—confirmation that the launch countdown had been initiated.

Almost at the same time, Lin's pistol barked. The bullet tore through Kim's right shoulder. He cried out and collapsed over the RFCU.

Kang momentarily froze as his mind tried to grasp what was happening.

Soo-Min, however, wasn't so slow. With a viper's speed, she drew a small revolver from a holster concealed under her bio-suit. There was no hesitation, no flicker of emotion on her sharp features.

CRACK.

The shot was precise, clinical. It was aimed at Lin's forehead but struck just below the left temple, possibly because Lin turned her head a fraction at the sound going off. There was no dramatic cry. Her body went rigid, then crumpled to the ground like a marionette with its strings cut.

The gunshot broke Kang's fugue. "Soo-Min!" he cried, a mixture of confusion and reprimand.

From his vantage point, Peter saw it all. He saw Lin fall. The world dissolved into a silent, dizzying nightmare. Every ounce of training, every protocol, evaporated.

"NO!" The roar was torn from his throat. "Echo Team! Go! Go! GO! Weapons free! Take them down!"

The warehouse erupted. The staccato thunder of automatic weapons fire replaced the silence. Muzzle flashes lit up the shadows like strobes. Peter's team, breaching from two points, engaged Kang's enforcers in a vicious, close-quarters firefight.

Kang grabbed his sister's arm. "We're leaving! Now!" They sprinted for a rear emergency exit, abandoning their men and the weapon.

"Kang and the woman are fleeing! West exit!" Peter yelled into his comms, already moving. He vaulted over a stack of crates, ignoring the rounds pinging off the metal around him, and charged after them.

He burst out the back door into a narrow, trash-strewn alley. A helicopter, its rotors already spinning up, was parked on a makeshift pad. Soo-Min was already at the open cabin door, scrambling inside. Kang was five yards behind her.

"KANG!" Peter bellowed, raising his rifle.

The helicopter pilot saw the armed man and lifted the

craft abruptly. Kang leaped for the skid. In that moment, he turned, his body twisting, placing himself between Peter's rifle and the escaping helicopter—a final, instinctive shield for his sister.

Peter fired twice.

The bullets struck Kang in the back and side, slamming him out of the air. He landed hard on the asphalt as the helicopter climbed away, Soo-Min's impassive face looking down from the cabin before it vanished over the roofline.

Peter ran to him, his boot rolling the man over. Kang was gasping, blood bubbling from his lips. His eyes, wide with shock and fading life, found Peter's. And in that moment, Peter saw it. As Kang's head lolled to the side, the hair above his ear fell away.

A fresh, surgical scar. Just like Clay's. Just like Asher's.

Kang choked out a wet, gurgling laugh. "We're ... just empty vessels Harrington. You're ... no different from me."

The light died in his eyes. The truth died with him.

Peter stood over him, frozen for a precious second, the words echoing in his soul. Then he remembered Lin. And the missile. He turned and sprinted back into the warehouse.

The firefight was still raging. Two of Kang's enforcers were using the missile's launch console as cover, trading fire with Echo Team. The digital readout on the console glowed red as the numbers ticked down: 06:47... 06:46 ...

"The countdown!" Peter roared, his voice cutting through the din. "It's active!"

"The igniter!" Kim screamed, clutching his bleeding shoulder. "It's at the top, in the propellant grain! The forward access panel!"

Peter's training seized control. He unclipped the worn leather sheath of his Leatherman from his belt. "Echo Team! Suppressing fire on my position! I need to get to that scaffolding! Everything you've got!"

The focus of the battle shifted instantly. His team laid down a devastating hail of fire, forcing the two enforcers near the console to duck behind it. Rounds sparked off the steel and concrete around Peter.

"Five minutes!" Kim yelled.

Peter sprinted in a low crouch toward the stack of maintenance scaffolding. "Echo-Four! With me!"

Another operative broke cover, providing suppressive fire as Peter grabbed the heavy structure. Together, they manhandled it, the metal feet screeching against the concrete. A burst of automatic fire ripped through the space between them.

"Four minutes!"

They slammed the scaffolding into place beside the elevated nose of the missile. A round spanged off the steel rail inches from Peter's head. He flinched but didn't stop, scrambling up the rungs.

"Echo-Two, I'm exposed on this platform! Keep them off me!" he yelled, the Leatherman already open in his palm. The forward access panel was secured by four flush-mounted bolts.

"Three minutes thirty seconds!"

Peter fitted the Phillips head bit and leaned his whole weight into it. The first bolt was stubborn. He could hear the distinct crack-thump of a sniper round from somewhere in the rafters punching into sheet metal.

"Three minutes! Sniper in the rafters! Find him!" Echo-Two's voice was strained over the comms.

The final bolt spun free. He pried the panel off with the tool's built-in pry bar, revealing the complex innards. Wires snaked around the central housing. There it was: the igniter, a blunt, cylindrical device seated deep into the heart of the solid fuel.

"Two minutes thirty! Disconnect the leads!" Kim shouted.

Peter snapped the Leatherman shut and reopened it, selecting the needle-nose pliers. His world narrowed to the tiny, shielded connectors. The firefight became a distant roar.

CRACK! Another sniper round, closer this time.

"Two minutes!"

Peter carefully squeezed the release tab on the first connector with the pliers. It came free with a soft click.

"One minute thirty!"

The second connector was wedged. He gripped it with the metal jaws, his knuckles white. He pulled. Nothing. He pulled again, a grunt of effort tearing from his throat.

"One minute!"

With a final, desperate wrench, the connector tore loose in a shower of plastic.

"Pull it out!"

Peter pocketed the Leatherman and wrapped both hands around the igniter's cold body. It was stuck fast.

"It's jammed!"

"Twist it! Twist and pull!"

He twisted, the metal grinding. A half-turn. It moved! He braced his feet and pulled with everything he had, his back muscles screaming.

From the corner of his eye, he saw one of his men, Echo-Four, stagger and fall near the warehouse entrance, hit by fire from the rafters. The covering fire from his team intensified, a desperate, last-stand fury.

With a final, metallic shriek, the igniter came free in his hands.

00:17 ... 00:16 ... 00:15 ...

He stumbled back on the platform, clutching the heavy cylinder.

"It didn't work!" he roared.

"Look!" Kim screamed, pointing.

A single line of text flashed on the board: IGNITER OF-FLINE. LAUNCH ABORT.

00:03 ... 00:02 ... 00:01 ... 00:00.

A single, mournful tone sounded, and the display died.

The gunfire didn't stop immediately. A final, enraged burst came from one of the last enforcers before he was cut down by a precise three-round burst from Echo-Two. Then, true silence fell, thick and heavy, broken only by the moans of the wounded and the ragged breathing of the survivors.

The missile stood inert. San Francisco was safe.

Peter stood on the scaffolding, the igniter a dead weight in his hand. He looked down at the body of Echo-Four, who had died to give him these last few seconds. Then his eyes found Lin.

He had won. He had saved millions.

But as he gazed at her still form on the concrete, the victory was a hollow, aching void. He sank down onto the metal grating, the igniter dropping from his numb fingers to clatter on the scaffold below, the sound a tiny, insignificant echo in the vast, unforgiving silence.

The left side of Lin's head was ripped open. Blood and brain had conjealed around the wound. Peter cradled her in his arms, rocking her like a baby as tears liberally flowed down his cheeks. "Oh Lin," he said, not caring about anything in the world. "Why? Why you?"

– 18 –

Dead Reckoning

Russian Doll Administrative Wing,
Platform Lazarus, Gulf of Thailand

PETER stood stiffly before Commander Crane, a million things running through his mind as he tried to control his emotions. Crane, for his part, seemed more tense than his usual self, a sign that he recognized this was no ordinary meeting, that there was a potential for it to go south. To this extent, he stayed close to his desk, close to the pistol that was secretly positioned there as a contingency.

Peter gazed at Crane, sensing the tension, but waited for Crane to speak first. Formality, even in these tense conditions, trumped personal egos.

Crane began, his voice a model of measured calm. "The initial after-action reports are in. You didn't just save millions of lives in the Bay Area, Peter. You saved an entire technological ecosystem, an industry that we need to stay ahead of the curve. The country owes you a debt it will never acknowledge."

Peter didn't blink. The words were empty, meaningless numerals in a ledger he wanted no part of. "But at what cost?" His voice was gravel, worn down by rage and grief. "The life of Lin Sijue. One of our most promising agents. One of the best people I've ever known. You lied to me, Crane. You're despicable."

Crane took the criticism with the even temper of a man who had expected nothing less. He steepled his fingers. "The world is not perfect, nor am I. I take full responsibility for Agent Sijue's death. Perhaps it was avoidable. But that's 20-20 hindsight. Without her intervention, the emotional leverage she had over Kang, we may have lost precious seconds that could have spelled the difference between success and disaster."

"But you said her cover was blown," Peter shot back, the memory of Crane's briefing in San Jose burning in his mind. "You told me you pulled her out of the loop precisely because of that. Then you broke your word and sent her back in."

"Yes," Crane admitted, his gaze unwavering. "I broke my word because I realized at the last minute that she could buy us time. She was given explicit instructions not to risk her life, to provide a distraction and then extract. Evidently, she didn't heed my advice."

"Your advice?" Peter took a half-step forward, his hands clenching into fists at his sides. "You think knowing what she knew about Kang, knowing his temperament, she could just walk in there and he wouldn't kill her? You sent her to her death."

"You seem to forget, Agent Harrington, that she was a highly trained female operative who had cultivated a deep, personal relationship with the target," Crane stated, his tone clinical. "That connection is an asset, just as important as bullets and intel. It was a calculated risk."

"You sacrificed her," Peter said, the truth of it cold and absolute. "Just like you sacrificed Asher, and Clay. What did you do with their originals, Crane? Decommission them? Archive their memories like faulty software?"

Crane's eyes narrowed slightly, the first crack in his placid facade. The question had hit its mark. "The originals are perfectly safe," he said, his voice dropping a degree. "They have been given new names, new identities. They're still on the Russian Doll payroll, comfortably retired. They will never be utilized in the field again."

"Unless you need something from them," Peter countered, the pieces clicking into a horrifying whole. "Some piece of personal information you failed to copy. Is that what happened with Clay? You failed to transpose the things he knew about me into his memory profile? That's why the clone was so erratic in Taipei."

Crane was silent for a long moment, then gave a single, curt nod. "A miscalibration in the emotional memory mapping. I made that mistake. There will always be unknowns. It's a matter of striking the right balance. I'm not looking to steal every intimate detail of a person's character. All I'm looking for is sufficient operational functionality."

"Robots," Peter quipped, the word dripping with contempt.

"Oh, they're more than robots," Crane replied, a flicker of fervent belief in his eyes. "They're the future. And your contribution to the program, Peter—both you and your duplicates—has been highly valued."

The admission was like a physical blow. It confirmed the utter commodification of everyone Crane commanded. "The cost," Peter said, his voice trembling with renewed fury, "is not worth it. Not to me." He drew himself up to his full height. "I formally tender my resignation. Effective immediately."

Crane stared at him coolly, the brief intensity gone, replaced by his usual calculating calm. "Why don't you just take a long holiday, Peter? You deserve it. You just saved the free world. When you calm down, you'll realize the sacrifice, as painful as it is, was worth it. I'm not going to endorse your resignation."

"I'm not giving you a choice." Peter's voice dropped to a low, dangerous register. He held up his left arm, pulling back the cuff of his jacket to reveal the faint, silvery line on his wrist. "You won't find me, ever again. And if you try to send another one of those things with my face, I'll be waiting for it."

Crane's eyes flickered to the scar. He didn't argue. Instead, he pressed a button on his intercom. "Justine. My office, please."

The door swung open moments later, and Justine Fairweather stepped in, her expression neutral, a slim file folder in her hand. "Peter," she said, her voice a calm counterpoint to the storm in the room.

She didn't go to Crane. She walked directly to Peter and offered him the file. "Here is your official documentation," she said, her eyes meeting his. "It absolves you of all Russian Doll responsibilities and grants you an honorable discharge, contingent on you being on extended, non-official leave. It's all there. Enjoy your freedom."

Peter was stunned. He looked from the folder to Crane, who allowed a thin, victorious smile to touch his lips.

"Take it, Peter," Crane said. "We've even added a clause that increases your holiday loading by thirty percent. I think you'll find the severance more than adequate."

For a moment, Peter was of a mind to take the papers and tear them to shreds. But then his eyes met Fairweather's again. He saw no malice there, only a quiet, insistent purpose. She gave a slight, almost imperceptible shake of her head. Take it.

He took the folder. It felt heavy, final.

Fairweather gently took his arm. "Come on," she said, her tone softening. "Let's get you out of here." She said it not as Crane's aide, but as a co-conspirator, and she guided him from the office before Crane could say another word.

The door clanked shut behind them, sealing Crane away. They walked in silence for a moment, the corridor stretching before them.

"You're a good man, Peter," Fairweather said quietly, not looking at him. "Believe it or not, Crane thinks of you like family. Remember, his son was killed on the North Korean border. He knows only too well what it means to lose a loved one. When he uses the word 'sacrifice,' he doesn't use it lightly. It's the entire reason he is so hell-bent on finding ways to avoid sacrificing real people."

"By turning us into lab rats and creating copies to die in our place?" Peter shot back, the memory of Crane's cold explanation fresh in his mind. "He didn't save Lin. He just copied her memories and sent a puppet to die. The Lin I loved is gone, and you've got a data file you think gives you the right to make more. It's like he wants me to be as bitter and empty as he is. To make his own loss make sense."

Fairweather stopped and turned to him, her gaze direct

and unwavering. "But you won't, will you?" she offered, a statement of fact. "You're better than him."

Peter looked down at the file in his hands, his ticket to a gilded cage. But he knew, with a cold certainty, that freedom was an illusion. Lin was gone, but the truth of what had been done to her—the mining of her mind, the system that had used her life as a script—was still active. The real Lin might be "safe" in some gilded cage, but the machine that had desecrated her past was still running.

He wasn't free. He was just changing the battlefield.

He met Fairweather's eyes again and gave a single, grim nod. The reckoning wasn't over. It had only just begun.

– 19 –

Human Unpredictability
Russian Doll Infirmary,
Platform Lazarus, Gulf of Thailand

CONSCIOUSNESS returned to Lin Sijue not as a sudden shock, but as a slow, reluctant tide. The first thing she registered was the absence of sensation—no straps, no pain, only the soft pressure of a mattress beneath her and the sterile, chilled air of a controlled environment. It was the air of Platform Lazarus.

She opened her eyes. The room was small, private, and featureless save for the bed and a single chair. A medical monitor glowed softly beside her, its screen a flatline of green. No IVs, no wires. They had sedated her for transport, and now they were done.

The door hissed open and Dr. Raskova stepped in, her

expression as unreadable as the data on her tablet. She didn't speak, merely took Lin's wrist to check her pulse, her fingers cold and impersonal. She shone a penlight into Lin's eyes, nodded to herself, and made a note on the tablet.

"Vitals are stable. Cognitive function appears nominal," Raskova said, not to Lin, but to the room. She turned and left without another word.

A moment later, the void she left was filled by Justine Fairweather.

Lin pushed herself up on her elbows, a groggy weakness making the motion difficult. "Justine," she rasped, her throat dry.

"Lin." Fairweather's smile was small, a carefully calibrated expression of warmth that didn't quite reach her eyes. She pulled the chair closer and sat. "How are you feeling?"

"Like I've been packed in ice and shipped as cargo." Lin's gaze was sharpening, cutting through the drug-induced fog. "What happened? The mission."

Fairweather's posture was perfect, her hands folded in her lap. "The mission was a success. The missile was disarmed. Kang is dead."

A wave of relief, so potent it was almost nauseating, washed over Lin. But it was immediately followed by a sharper, more personal fear. "And Peter?"

"Peter did a great job," Fairweather said, her tone smooth and reassuring. "He decommissioned the missile. Saved everyone."

Lin's eyes searched Fairweather's face, looking for the crack, the tell. "So he's alive? He's safe?" The question was simple, but for Lin, after the warehouse, after the clones, after everything, it was the only question that mattered.

"Yes," Fairweather said, her gaze steady. "He's perfectly fine. He's been rewarded with extended leave. He needs time to decompress, and we've given him a very generous package."

Lin let out a breath she didn't realize she'd been holding, sinking back into the pillow. He was alive. He was safe. The two pillars of her world, for a moment, felt solid again.

Then, the next, inevitable thought surfaced. "Will I be able to see him?"

Fairweather's features creased with a look of profound, practiced sympathy. "I'm afraid not. Not until we determine what Black Hand's next move will be. The network is still active. We need you to stay on track for us. Can you do that?"

The words were a bucket of cold water. Stay on track. It was Crane's phrase. The relief evaporated, replaced by a familiar, cold agitation. She pushed herself fully upright, swinging her legs over the side of the bed, facing Fairweather fully. The grogginess was gone, burned away by a sudden, clarifying anger.

"Are you in on all this with Crane?" Lin asked, her voice

low.

Fairweather didn't flinch. "I used to be a field agent, just like you. But Crane felt I was more useful to him in the office. I don't know why, but the glove seems to fit." She paused, choosing her words with evident care. "He doesn't, however, tell me about every plan he's got going on. It's a complex operation, and I just get to see part of it."

"Which part?" Lin pressed, her eyes narrowing.

"I handle the rendering of new identities for… retired agents. That's my main task. And I do a few other administrative jobs, but they're not relevant to you."

"New identities," Lin repeated, the phrase landing with the weight of a tombstone. "Is that what happened to Dustin Asher and Sebastian Clay?"

Fairweather gave a single, solemn nod.

A cold dread coiled in Lin's stomach. "Is that what is going to happen to Peter and me?"

This time, Fairweather hesitated. Her composure flickered. But Lin's eyes were on her, deploring, demanding the truth.

"Eventually, yes," Fairweather admitted softly. "But not for now. You have nothing to worry about at this point."

"What if I want to see Peter?" Lin's voice was tight, a thread of desperation woven through the steel. "Can I see him?"

"Not right now," Fairweather said, her tone firming up.

"As I said, he's on extended leave."

"But after," Lin insisted, leaning forward. "After all this is over."

"I'm not sure," Fairweather replied, a wall of bureaucratic finality in her words. "It's not my jurisdiction."

The disappointment was a physical ache, quickly metastasizing into a hot, sharp anger. "Then you're just as bad as Crane," Lin spat.

Fairweather took the blow without a change in expression. She absorbed the accusation, her own gaze seeming to grow weary. "Perhaps I am," she replied, her voice barely a whisper. "But you know I would never do anything to hurt you or Peter. You do understand that, don't you?"

"Prove it then," Lin challenged, her body tense, poised for a fight that wasn't physical.

A veiled, almost sad laugh escaped Fairweather's lips. "Prove it, how?"

"Let me go. Let me go right now."

Fairweather's eyebrows rose in genuine surprise. "Why would I do that?"

"Because I promised someone I would help rescue their family," Lin said, her voice dropping to an intense, fervent whisper. "And I always keep my promises."

A knowing look dawned on Fairweather's face. "You mean Kim Seong-Jin's family."

"Yes."

Fairweather nodded slowly, as if a long-held suspicion had just been confirmed. "You couldn't live with yourself if you broke your promise. I know you well enough to know you will find a way to do it, even if Crane tries to stop you."

Lin said nothing. Her silent, unwavering stare was confirmation enough.

"In that case," Fairweather said, her voice dropping to a conspiratorial murmur, "there's something I need to tell you." She leaned in closer. "Peter only killed Kang's clone in San Francisco. We don't know where the real Kang is."

Lin absorbed this, her face a mask. She showed a flicker of surprise, but it was a calculated performance. "I suspected as much," she admitted. "There was something wrong about him after Bok transferred the missile to the Celestial Phoenix. I had seen the signs in the Peter clones..."

"We have Kim Seong-Jin in a safe place," Fairweather continued. "He was wounded when Peter's team attacked the warehouse, but he's okay."

"Where is he?"

"Bangkok."

Bangkok. The main hub for North Korean escapees. The unspoken gateway. Lin nodded, the entire plan crystallizing in her mind. "Then let me go to him."

Fairweather studied her for a long, tense moment. The hum of the platform's life support was the only sound. Finally, she spoke. "I'm going to do something now that can get me in a lot of trouble. So you have to promise me this never happened. Okay?"

"Sure," Lin said, her heart beginning to hammer against her ribs.

Fairweather reached into the pocket of her impeccably tailored trousers. She didn't look around; her trust, or her recklessness, was absolute. She pressed a small, cold, magnetic key card into Lin's palm.

"This is the access key to Crane's private one-man sub. It's docked at Bay 7, maintenance sector. It's fully charged and ready to go. The logs will be wiped. You were never here."

Lin's fingers closed around the key. It felt like a bridge to an unknown land. The image of herself getting lost in that land, alone, brought back the memory of her grandmother's prayer wheel, confiscated by Quinn and now locked away in his lab somewhere. It was a piece of her soul held hostage by the very machine she was escaping. Its absence was a physical hole in her heart. She looked at Fairweather with an unspoken ache. She couldn't blame her, she wouldn't understand. How could she?

"Thank you, Justine."

"Don't thank me," Fairweather said, standing up and smoothing her trousers. "Just go. And remember … you never saw me."

She turned and walked out, the door hissing shut behind

her, leaving Lin alone with a key, a promise, and the terrifying, exhilarating taste of freedom.

– 20 –

The Tumen Crossing
Yanji
Chinese-North Korea Border

THE familiar scent of mildew and stale air greeted Lin as she pushed open the door to the Thonburi safe house. It was a scent that had once meant tension and secrecy with Peter. Now, it was just empty.

Kim Seong-Jin started violently from a worn armchair, a book tumbling from his lap. His face, which had been etched with a permanent state of worry, contorted into pure, unvarnished shock. He stumbled back a step, his hand flying to his chest.

"You …" he stammered, his eyes wide with a superstitious dread. "You are dead. I saw it. The blood … your head …"

"It wasn't me," Lin said, her voice low and steady as she closed the door. She kept her distance, giving him space to process the impossible. "The woman you saw die in that warehouse was a copy. A clone. Her name was EVE-7."

Kim stared, his mind visibly struggling to reconcile the memory of violent death with the living woman before him. "A … clone? Like the Peter Harrington copies?"

"Yes. Crane's project. Matryoshka." The word felt like a curse on her tongue. "The real me was … in storage. Now I'm back. But no one can know, Kim. Not Peter, not anyone. This stays between us. Do you understand?"

The sheer, chilling absurdity of the truth seemed to overwhelm his initial fear. He gave a slow, dazed nod, the fight-or-flight tension seeping from his shoulders, replaced by a weary acceptance of a world that had lost all its rules. "I understand."

He told her everything then. With Kang's catastrophic failure in San Francisco, his star had fallen within Black Hand. The mastermind, Bok, had reasserted control. As part of Kang's demotion, the leverage against Kim—his wife Yoona and his daughters, Hana and Min-Ji—had been deemed a low-priority asset. They had been moved from a high-security political prison to a re-education camp near Hoeryong, in the far north. It was a slight improvement in conditions, but a death sentence by inches.

"But there is a chance," Kim said, a fragile hope lighting

his eyes. "A message. Smuggled out through a guard who can be bribed. Yoona … she is clever. She says they will try to cross the Tumen River. Near Yanji. My cousin, Dong-Hyun, he has a shop there. He can receive them."

Lin didn't hesitate. "Then we go. Now."

The landscape in Yanji was a stark, frozen contrast to Bangkok's humid chaos. A bitter wind scoured the streets, carrying the scent of coal smoke and frozen earth. Kim Dong-Hyun was a younger, quieter version of his cousin, with a shopkeeper's cautious eyes that missed nothing. He confirmed the plan in hushed tones over cups of bitter tea.

"The message came last night. They will try tonight. The moon is almost gone. The cold is bad, but the ice is thick. It is the best chance they will get."

While Kim Seong-Jin, agitated and hopeful, went to scout the specific stretch of riverbank, to see the ice for himself and trace the path his family would take in his mind, Lin turned to Dong-Hyun.

"I need two more things," she said, her voice dropping below the hum of the shop's heating unit. "And my friend cannot know."

Dong-Hyun's eyes narrowed, assessing her. "What things?"

"A rifle. And an identity. A North Korean one."

He was silent for a long moment, then gave a single, sharp nod. "It will cost."

"Money is not a problem."

He led her out the back, through a maze of alleys crusted with dirty ice. Their first stop was a small, struggling photographic studio. The air inside smelled of chemicals and dust. Lin sat for a grim, passport-sized photo, her face arranged into a mask of blank deference. The forger, a man with ink-stained fingers, worked with practiced efficiency, laminating her new life onto a cardstock ID. Lin paid in crisp American dollars.

Next, they visited a taciturn farmer on the city's outskirts. From a hidden compartment in his barn, the man produced a well-worn Type 81 hunting rifle and a box of cartridges. It was no military sniper system, but it was accurate and reliable. Lin handled the transaction with a cold professionalism that made Dong-Hyun watch her with a new, wary respect. She paid the man, slung the rifle in a cloth bag, and turned to Dong-Hyun.

"You will not speak of this to your cousin," she said. It was not a question.

"He is my family," Dong-Hyun replied, a flicker of conflict in his eyes.

"And I am the one who will make sure his family reaches him alive tonight. My business after that is my own. His concern would only put them in danger. Do we understand each other?"

He held her gaze, then looked away, defeated by her iron

resolve. "We understand each other."

That night, the cold was a physical presence, biting through layers of clothing. The only sound on the Chinese bank was the groan of the ice and the whisper of the wind. Kim Seong-Jin trembled, though not from the cold, his eyes fixed on the impenetrable darkness of the opposite shore. Dong-Hyun stood ready with thick blankets and a thermos of sweet tea.

Lin was apart from them, a statue in the shadows. She had assembled the rifle, the metallic clicks unnaturally loud in the silence. She rested the stock on a fallen log, her eye pressed to the scope. The world narrowed to a green-tinted circle of night vision. She scanned the North Korean bank, tracing the predictable path of a distant patrol, her finger resting on the cold metal of the safety. She was a guardian ghost, a silent promise of violence held in abeyance.

Then, movement.

Three figures, small and dark against the snow, emerged from the treeline. They moved with a desperate, shuffling haste onto the vast, white plain of the frozen river.

"There," Kim Seong-Jin breathed, the word a prayer.

Lin tracked them. Every stumble, every hesitant pause, sent a jolt of adrenaline through her. She could see the lead figure—Yoona, she presumed—urging the two smaller ones forward. The distance seemed infinite. Her muscles ached with the tension of holding still, her world defined by the crosshairs and the three fragile lives moving through them.

A searchlight on the North Korean side flicked on, a blinding white eye sweeping the landscape. Lin's finger slid from the safety to the trigger. The light swept past, then swung back, slower this time. It crept toward the river. Toward the figures.

Kim gasped.

Lin exhaled, slow and controlled. The center of the scope found the glowing orb of the light. She calculated the drop, the wind. She began the gentle, steady pressure on the trigger.

Then, the light swept away, continuing its monotonous patrol. The guard had seen nothing. The moment passed.

The rest was an agony of slow motion. Finally, the three figures, half-frozen and exhausted, scrambled up the Chinese bank. Kim Seong-Jin rushed forward, enveloping them in a silent, sobbing embrace, muffling their cries against his coat. Dong-Hyun swiftly wrapped them in blankets.

It was over. They were safe.

Kim turned to Lin, his face a mess of tears and radiant joy. "Lin … how can I ever … We must go, we must get them warm."

He expected her to lower the rifle, to join them, to share in the victory.

Instead, she stood, slinging the rifle over her shoulder.

From her pack, she pulled the humble, drab joseon-ot she had acquired. She began to change, right there on the riverbank, her modern clothes disappearing under the traditional North Korean dress.

"What are you doing?" Kim asked, his joy turning to confusion, then to dawning horror.

"My mission isn't over," Lin said, her voice calm and final. She tucked her hair under a plain headscarf and showed him the fake ID. "Kang is still alive. And he's in there."

"No! You can't! It is suicide!"

"It is a debt," she corrected him. She looked at Yoona, at the two young girls clinging to their mother, their eyes wide with fear and confusion. "A promise I made to myself. Live well, Kim Seong-Jin. Your family is free. Now it's my turn."

Before he could form another word of protest, she turned and walked back down the bank onto the ice. She did not look back. The wind snatched at her rough-spun clothes as she retraced the path of freedom in reverse, a single, purposeful figure moving against the tide.

When her boots crunched on the snow of the North Korean shore, she did not pause. She moved quickly to a stacked pile of firewood near the treeline, shoved the rifle deep into its heart, and covered the hole. Stripped of her weapon, she pulled the scarf tighter around her face, bowed her head, and shuffled into the shadows of a footpath.

In moments, Lin Sijue was gone. She had become just another anonymous woman in the darkness, her eyes already scanning the grim landscape for the trail of her prey. The hunt had begun.

– 21 –

The House Always Wins
Pyongyang Casino
Yanggakdo International Hotel, Pyongyang

THE Yanggakdo International Hotel rose from the silt of the Taedong River like a concrete tombstone, its circular form a futile attempt at modernity in a city starved of light. For three nights, Lin had haunted its periphery, a ghost in the drab clothing of a low-level functionary. Her world had narrowed to the scent of damp coal smoke, the taste of cold noodles from a street vendor, and the fixed point of the casino's service entrance.

The intel had cost her the last of the cash Dong-Hyun had given her—a whispered transaction with a kitchen scullion who smelled of grease and fear. The failed one, the man had called Kang. He gambles. He loses. He drinks his shame. He uses the back door now.

So Lin waited. She became a student of the hotel's nocturnal rhythms, the comings and goings of party elites and their minders. She was a shadow, her borrowed North Korean identity a flimsy shield, her entire being focused on the single, burning point of her vengeance.

On the fourth night, the service door swung open, spilling a trapezoid of jaundiced light onto the wet asphalt. And he was there.

Kang Hyuk stumbled out, a solitary figure shorn of his enforcers, his power, his terrifying grace. His fine suit was rumpled, a dark stain spreading on his silk tie. He braced himself against the wall, head bowed, his shoulders slumped in a posture of defeat so profound it was almost pitiable.

Lin felt nothing. The pity was a reflex, instantly incinerated in the furnace of her memory: the feel of his grip, the smell of soju, the sound of the clone's head hitting the warehouse floor. This was not the fanatical revolutionary or the cunning predator. This was the man underneath—a hollowed-out shell of pride and failure.

She moved from the shadows without a sound, her footsteps swallowed by the distant hum of the city's generators. She stopped ten feet from him, a specter made flesh.

"The house always wins, Kang Hyuk," she said, her voice low and flat in the chilly air.

He jerked upright, his eyes, bleary and bloodshot, struggling to focus. For a moment, there was only confusion. Then, recognition dawned, slow and horrifying. He saw the woman he had violated, the asset he had trusted, the ghost he had ordered killed in San Francisco.

"You…" he slurred, pushing himself off the wall. A flicker of his old arrogance returned, a defense against the impossible. "You are dead."

"The one you knew was a copy," Lin said, taking a step closer. Her hands were empty, held loosely at her sides. "Just like the one you sent to die in San Francisco. Crane's little trick. You were playing with dolls, Kang. But I am real."

The truth landed, dismantling his remaining composure. His face contorted, a mess of drunken rage and shattered pride. "You betrayed me! You ruined everything!"

"You ruined yourself," Lin countered, her voice still chillingly calm. "Your grand crusade failed. Your bioweapon was disarmed. Your sister ran. And Bok Yeong left you here to rot in a Pyongyang casino, drowning the shame of your failure."

Each word was a precise, surgical strike. Kang let out a raw, animal cry of fury and lunged at her. It was a clumsy, telegraphed move, devoid of the lethal skill he'd once possessed. Lin didn't flinch. She sidestepped, letting his momentum carry him past her. As he stumbled, she drove the rigid point of two fingers deep into the nerve cluster just below his ear.

He grunted, his body seizing for a split second before collapsing to his knees, gagging.

Lin stood over him. This was not the dramatic, explosive death he might have envisioned. It was quiet, ignominious, a squalid end in a back alley. She reached into the folds of her coat and withdrew a simple, brutal tool: a ice pick, its tip filed to a vicious point, procured from the same black market that had supplied her ID.

Kang looked up, his eyes wide with a final, sobering terror. He saw no rage in her face, only a cold, absolute resolve. There was no "Maya Chan" left. This was Lin Sijue, reclaiming what he had taken.

"This is for me," she whispered.

She didn't stab him. She placed the point against the base of his skull, right where the neural implant scar would be on a clone. Then, with a single, powerful thrust, she drove it up and into his brain.

There was a sharp, wet sound. His body stiffened, then went limp, slumping to the ground in a heap of expensive fabric and broken ambition.

Lin didn't watch him die. She was already turning, wiping the pick clean on her trousers before discarding it into a storm drain. She melted back into the shadows, leaving the architect of a million deaths to his solitary, meaningless end in the Pyongyang dark. The first part of her vow was fulfilled.

But as she disappeared into the sleeping city, a new, more dangerous hunt was already beginning. Across town, in a sterile government lab, a secure line rang. Dr. Soo-Min Kang, reviewing the genetic decay rates of the San Francisco bio-agent, answered it. The voice on the other end was frantic, describing a body, an ice pick, a woman fitting a certain description seen lurking near the Yanggakdo.

Soo-Min listened, her face a mask of cold stone. When the caller finished, she simply said, "Secure the scene. Tell no one else."

She hung up, her hands trembling not with grief, but with a pure, incandescent rage. Her brother was a fool, but he was her fool. And the impostor, the whore who had caused all of this, was not dead after all. She was here.

Soo-Min's mind, brilliant and methodical, began to calculate. The impostor had a single logical escape route: back the way she came. The Tumen River crossing. She opened a map on her screen, her finger tracing the border near Yanji. She would not fail as her brother had. She would not be reckless.

She would be a scientist hunting a specimen. And she would exterminate it.

– 22 –

The Hunter's Price
Yanji
Chinese-North Korea Border

THE silence of the North Korean countryside was a lie. It was not peaceful, but watchful. Every creak of a cart, every distant bark of a dog, felt like an accusation. Lin had moved like a phantom for days, hitchhiking in the beds of military trucks, walking through frozen fields at night, her senses stretched to a razor's edge.

Killing Kang had been too easy. It felt less like an ending and more like a transaction. The real settlement, she knew in her bones, was still outstanding. Kang was the passion, the bluster. But Soo-Min was the intellect, the cold, enduring will. Lin had not just killed her brother; she had invalidated her life's work, humiliated her in front of Bok Yeong.

A woman like Soo-Min would not let that stand. Kang was the bait. The trap was yet to be sprung.

The small village near the crossing was a cluster of low buildings huddled against the relentless wind. The air smelled of woodsmoke and frozen earth. Lin, her face smudged with dirt and her body aching with a fatigue that went deeper than muscle, slipped into a cramped gukjip. The warmth from the single stove was a physical shock. She kept her head down, ordering a bowl of noodles with a mumbled dialect she'd practiced, her eyes constantly scanning the single room in the reflection of a darkened window.

She was halfway through the bowl, forcing the warm broth down, when she saw it. A black sedan, impossibly clean and official, pulled up silently outside. The door opened, and a figure emerged, swaddled in a long, dark coat, her posture rigid and precise.

Soo-Min.

She didn't look around wildly. Her gaze, like a scalpel, swept the scene and immediately landed on Lin through the steamy window. There was no surprise in it, only the cold satisfaction of a hypothesis confirmed.

Lin didn't wait. She was up and moving, overturning the table with a crash that sent bowls shattering across the floor. She burst out of a rear door into an alley, the startled cries of the owner fading behind her. The hunt was on.

She didn't run for the river. That was the expected path. Instead, she led Soo-Min on a twisting chase through the village's back ways. As she ran, a memory surfaced, sharp and unbidden: the weight of her grandmother's prayer wheel in her hand, the smooth, familiar spin of it. Now it was gone, locked in Quinn's lab, another part of her soul held captive by Crane's machine. This confrontation with another ruthless woman felt like a dark echo of that sacred storm, a perversion of the strength her grandmother represented.

The first crack of thunder rolled in the distance, a low growl that promised violence. The wind picked up, biting and raw.

She was a fox, using every scrap of cover. Soo-Min was a wolf, methodical and relentless, never gaining, but never falling behind. A shot rang out, the crack of a pistol, splintering wood a foot from Lin's head. Soo-Min wasn't trying to capture her.

Lin broke for the tree line at the edge of the village, the frozen river glittering in the distance. Her plan was simple: get to the woodpile, get the rifle, and end this. But Soo-Min knew the terrain, or was simply that good. She cut a parallel path, her longer strides closing the distance as they entered the sparse woods.

Lin felt the impact before she heard the second shot—a searing, white-hot pain in her side. It wasn't a clean hit; it was a graze, but it was deep enough to tear a cry from her throat and send her stumbling. She crashed through brittle undergrowth, her hand clamped to her ribs, feeling the warm seep of blood through her layers.

She could see it now—the familiar, jumbled pile of logs by the riverbank, the Chinese side a hazy promise beyond the ice. Freedom was two hundred meters away. Above, the sky had turned the color of a fresh bruise, and the first fat, heavy flakes of snow began to fall.

Soo-Min emerged from the trees, pistol raised, her breath pluming in the air. "There is no escape for a disease," she called out, her voice cutting through the wind. "You are a contagion. I am the cure."

Lin dove behind the woodpile as a third shot thudded into the frozen logs. The world narrowed to the scent of pine, the coppery taste of blood in her mouth, and the frantic scraping of her fingers through the icy gaps between the logs. Where is it? Where—

Her numb fingers closed around the cold, familiar shape of the rifle's stock. She dragged it out, the old hunting weapon feeling alien and clumsy in her hands compared to the custom tools of Russian Doll.

Soo-Min was advancing, a dark silhouette against the snow. "You took everything from me!" she screamed, the clinical facade finally shattering into raw grief.

Lin fumbled with the bolt, her fingers stiff with cold. It

jammed. She wrestled with it, her heart hammering against her ribs.

A fourth shot. Wood splinters stung her face. Soo-Min was twenty meters away now, and closing.

Click. The bolt slid home.

At that moment, the sky split open. A fork of lightning illuminated the scene in a stark, blinding tableau—Soo-Min's face, twisted in hate; the snow-laden trees; the glint of the river. The immediate, world-shaking crack of thunder that followed was like the slam of a celestial door.

Lin rose, the rifle stock pressed against her cheek. Soo-Min saw the movement and fired again, the round whipping past Lin's ear. But Lin's world had gone still. There was no wind, no pain, no fear. There was only the front sight post, settling on the center mass of the woman who had armed the weapon that would have killed millions, the sister of the man who had broken her.

She exhaled halfway and squeezed the trigger.

The crack of the rifle was a final, definitive period, swallowed by the rolling echo of the thunder. Soo-Min was thrown backward, a dark flower blooming on her chest. She landed in the snow, her eyes wide with shock, staring at the storm-wracked sky, her pistol lying useless beside her.

Lin didn't watch. She worked the bolt, ejecting the spent cartridge, and slung the rifle over her shoulder. Clutching her bleeding side, she stumbled out from behind the woodpile and onto the ice of the Tumen River.

The storm had concealed her deadly encounter with Soo-Min from the guard tower in the distance. It would conceal her crossing, so long as she timed it between lightening bolts.

Each step was agony, a trail of crimson dots marking her path across the frozen expanse. She didn't look back. The storm her grandmother had promised was now hers, a power she had harnessed and survived. She kept her eyes on the far bank, on the shadowy figure of Kim Dong-Hyun waiting there. She had paid the river's price in blood and trauma. She had settled all her debts.

As her boots crunched on the gravel of the Chinese shore, she finally allowed herself to sway, the strength draining from her legs. Strong hands caught her before she fell. She had crossed over. She was free. But as Kim Dong-Hyun bundled her into a waiting truck, the face that swam in her vision was not his, nor Kang's, nor Soo-Min's.

It was Commander Crane's. And she knew, with a certainty as cold as the river she had just crossed, that her war was far from over.

– 23 –

The Last Russian Doll

Platform Lazarus, Gulf of Thailand

THE UN inspection helicopter, marked with stark white letters, was an alien bird descending upon the sterile secrecy of Platform Lazarus. Inside, Lin Sijue sat beside a seasoned, skeptical inspector named Almeida. Her evidence—the charred data stick from Asher, Kim Seong-Jin's testimony, and her own devastating account—had been enough to trigger a provisional, no-notice inspection. Crane's political armor was strong, but not impervious to a potential bioweapon and human cloning scandal.

As predicted, Crane's welcome was coldly cordial. But when Almeida's team moved beyond the sanctioned areas, towards the submerged laboratory wings, the atmosphere shattered.

"They're heading for the core containment," Fairweather's tense voice came over Crane's private comm. "They're not bluffing, sir."

Crane's face hardened. He gave a single, grim nod to Agent Martinez. "Contain the situation. Neutralize the inspection team. This is a hostile incursion."

Alarms blared. The staccato burst of automatic fire echoed through the corridors as Martinez's security team engaged the UN guards. In the ensuing chaos, Lin melted away from the firefight. This was the distraction she needed.

She moved with a vengeful purpose, descending into the heart of the platform. She found the cloning lab first—rows of amniotic tanks holding formless, growing things. She didn't hesitate, smashing control consoles with a fire axe, triggering emergency purges that filled the room with acrid smoke. She moved to the neural imprinting suite, the place where her memories had been stolen. She shattered the neural mappers, the servers labeled LAZARUS CORE, and ignited a chemical fire that began to race through the oxygen-rich environment.

Her final stop was Quinn's lab. She found him cowering behind a console, the fire spreading rapidly.

"The prayer wheel," Lin demanded, the axe in her hand leaving no room for negotiation.

"Quinn, dying from smoke, pointed a trembling finger towards a locked specimen drawer. "The… combination…" he gasped, before succumbing to the smoke.

Lin smashed the lock. Inside, nestled on a velvet tray, was her grandmother's prayer wheel. The relief that washed over her was profound, a piece of her soul instantly restored. As she clutched it, a final console screen flickered with an automated message: CRITICAL SYSTEMS FAILURE. INITIATING SATELLITE DATA BURST. MATRYOSHKA SEED VAULTED. LAZARUS LIVES.

The war was not over. But this battle was.

She fought her way back through the smoke and chaos towards the landing pad. Crane, realizing the scale of the destruction, was there, directing a team to shoot down the fleeing UN helicopter.

"Sir, the woman, Sijue… she's on the comm," Martinez said, handing him a headset.

Lin's voice, calm and clear, cut through the static and the roar of the flames. "It's over, Crane. The world is watching now. Shoot down this bird, and you're not a patriot protecting secrets anymore. You're a mass murderer. There's no coming back from that."

Crane stood frozen, his finger hovering over the comms button that would give the kill order. He saw the inferno consuming his life's work. He saw the resolve in Lin's transmission. To destroy her now would be a purely personal act of vengeance, and it would burn every last bridge he had.

With a roar of pure, impotent fury, he smashed the headset on the deck. "Let them go!" he bellowed.

The UN helicopter lifted away from the burning platform. Lin watched from the window as Platform Lazarus, the gilded cage and factory of nightmares, was consumed by the very fire it was built to contain. She had paid her debts, reclaimed her past, and struck a crippling blow. But as the satellite carrying the ghost of Lazarus sailed silently overhead in the void, she knew her work was not yet done. She held the prayer wheel tight. The storm had passed, but the sky was never truly clear.

– 24 –

New Memories

Amalfi Coast, Italy

THE sun was a bleeding orange wound on the horizon, painting the Tyrrhenian Sea in hues of fire and gold. Peter Harrington sat on the balcony of a cliffside café, the salt-kissed air a balm he was still learning to accept. In his hand was a week-old international newspaper, its headline vague but telling: "Mysterious Fire Destroys Derelict Oil Platform; Covert Terrorist Cell Suspected." He allowed himself a small, grim smile. He knew the truth behind the sanitized words.

He took a slow sip of his drink, the ice clinking softly. This was peace. It was fragile, unfamiliar, and haunted by a ghost he could not forget. He had spent weeks here, trying to bury the image of Lin's body in that San Francisco warehouse, the memory a shard of ice in his heart.

A figure moved at the edge of his vision, a silhouette approaching along the cobblestone path, backlit by the dazzling sunset. Something primal and deep within him stirred, a tremor that had nothing to do with conscious thought. The hairs on the back of his neck stood up. His breath hitched. It was a trick of the light, a cruel mirage born of grief and wishful thinking.

His mind, conditioned by betrayal and loss, supplied the cold, logical answer: *EVE-7. An impostor. Crane's final, vicious joke.*

She walked toward his table, her form shimmering in the halo of the sun. She stopped before him, and the light framed her face. It was her. Every detail was perfect. It was impossible.

Peter stood slowly, his chair scraping against the stone. His heart was a frantic drum against his ribs, a war between desperate hope and hardened suspicion. He searched her eyes, looking for the cold emptiness of the clone, the artifice.

His voice was a hoarse, guarded whisper. "Monte Cristo."

Her smile was small, a little sad, and held a universe of shared pain and secrets. "Temple Storm."

The codes were correct. The cadence was hers. But the doubt was a cage he couldn't escape. "How do I know," he asked, his voice trembling with the effort to hold back, "this isn't another one of Crane's tricks?"

Lin didn't answer with words. She stepped forward, closed the distance between them, and kissed him.

It was not the kiss of a programmed replica. It was not a performance. It was fierce, and tender, and alive with the raw, unscripted truth of everything they had survived. It tasted of salt, and sunset, and a forgiveness he didn't know he needed. It was a homecoming.

When they broke apart, Peter knew. He knew in his soul, in his bones, in the way his entire being settled into a peace he thought was lost forever. He rested his forehead against hers.

"But I saw you die," he breathed, the memory finally losing its power over him.

"You saw an impostor die," she corrected softly. "Not me."

He had to ask. "What about Crane?"

Lin demurred, a shadow passing behind her eyes. "Maybe he cloned himself. But for now, he's out of our hair." She chose not to mention Justine Fairweather, the final, ambiguous fate of the woman who had saved her, a secret she would carry alone.

She looked out at the darkening sea, then back to him. "Lazarus held our memories. Those are all gone now." She took his hand, her grip firm and real. "We are free to make new ones."

A slow, cheeky smile spread across Peter's face, the first genuine one in a long, long time. "You mean you never have to kill me again?"

Lin looked into his eyes, her own sparkling with a light that was entirely her own. "Not unless you piss me off."

And as the last sliver of sun vanished below the horizon, Peter Harrington knew that their long night was finally over. A new day was theirs to write, together.